*S*pirits
*Be*tween the Bays
Series

Volume **II**

Opening the Door

**Ghost
Stories by**

Ed Okonowicz

Spirits Between the Bays
Volume II
Opening the Door
Second Edition

Copyright 2003 by Edward M. Okonowicz Jr.
All rights reserved.

ISBN 1-890690-11-2

No portion of this book may be reproduced, in any form,
except for brief passages for review purposes, without written
permission from the author.

Published by
Myst and Lace Publishers
1386 Fair Hill Lane
Elkton, Maryland 21921

Visit our web site at
www.mystandlace.com

Printed in the U.S.A.
by Victor Graphics

Typography, Design and Illustrations
by Kathleen Okonowicz

Dedications

To my children
Theresa, Eddie and Mark
With all my thanks, affection and pride.
Ed Okonowicz

To my children Suzanne and Cassandra
You are the joy of my life.
Kathleen Burgoon Okonowicz

Acknowledgments

The author and illustrator appreciate the assistance of those who have played an important role in this project.

Special thanks are extended to:

Genevieve L. Alexander
for her unique insight and the professional skills she shared;

Hazel Brittingham, Mike Dixon, Dorothy Hudson,
Laura Overturf, Sande Warren Price,
George Reynolds and Gary Wyatt
for important leads and historical information;

Boni Nash and Kathlene Stegura
for their technical expertise;

and

John Brennan
Sue Moncure
Ted Stegura
and Monica Witkowski
for their proofreading and suggestions.

Also available from Myst and Lace Publishers, Inc.

Spirits Between the Bays Series

DelMarVa Murder Mystery Series

Stairway over the Brandywine

Possessed Possessions

Possessed Possessions 2

Disappearing Delmarva

Terrifying Tales of the Beaches and Bays

Terrifying Tales 2 of the Beaches and Bays

Ghosts

Matt Zabitka: Sports

Table of Contents

✤*The individuals involved have agreed to allow real names and actual locations to be used in this presentation of the story.*

Legends and Lore

Introduction

Thank you for deciding to read *Opening the Door*, the second book in the *Spirits Between the Bays* series originally published in 1995. This book has been out of print for two years, and we decided to release this second edtion, which includes several new stories along with all the tales and legends that were featured in the original version of the book.

Since the release in 1994 of *Pulling Back the Curtain*, our first volume of ghost books featuring unexplained events occurring between the Chesapeake and Delaware Bays, the stories have kept coming and never stopped. Over the years, we have had a number of interesting leads. While many have been offered during book signings, ghost tours and cemetery walks, others have been received through letters, phone calls and e-mail messages. And while most of the suggested stories have been spooky and eerie, a few of them have been horrifying and some even humorous.

For example, soon after *Pulling Back the Curtain's* release, several people called from housing developments identified in some of those stories, requesting the exact addresses of the haunted homes.

I asked each caller his or her address, and every person was relieved when assured their particular home was not featured in any of the tales in Volume I. (I really don't know what I would have said if the caller had lived in one of the actual haunted houses of which I had written. I'll deal with that problem when it arises.)

While I had expected this type of inquiry, I was surprised when a young woman called asking for the address of the residence of the Headless Horseman of Welsh Tract Church.

She explained that she had put down a deposit and signed a contract to buy a home located on Welsh Tract Road, south of Newark, Del.—the official, historical stomping ground of headless Charlie Miller and his white steed. The woman said the property settlement was scheduled within two weeks, but, if I told her the house she had selected was haunted, she was going to cancel the agreement and remain in her apartment.

I assured her that Charlie Miller was a non-threatening, out-of-doors variety of headless spirit, a restless fellow who dwelled strictly in the nearby woods and meadows—and every now and then had been sighted galloping along the I-95 median strip. I recommended that she go ahead with her settlement and move in her new home without fear—of headless Charlie, at least.

She gave out a sigh of relief so huge that I could almost see her reaction over the phone.

Another common question I am asked is: "Where do you find these stories?"

The answer is simple: "From people like you."

Although everyone has a story to tell, few people are willing to call or write even a very short note. To share a ghost story takes some effort and a large amount of trust. As a writer, I feel the contacts I have made with people who decided to tell me their experiences, or the stories they have heard, are the most satisfying part of this whole project.

It's been a joy to talk with each person and to get to know them, whether face to face or through phone conversations.

And the stories have come from everywhere.

But of all the calls, one of the most unusual was from a woman who heard an early morning interview program on WVUD-FM radio—the voice of the University of Delaware in Newark.

I was being interviewed by student DJ Bob Boudwin. When we went off the air, he got a final call from a woman who wanted to get in touch with me to share a ghost story.

The contact was unusual because she worked at the nearby Chrysler automobile assembly plant, testing car radios. Just by chance, one was tuned to the campus station's frequency. She heard the conversation we were having about ghosts and called to get my phone number. We later were able to meet, and she shared a very interesting ghost story that appeared in a future volume of this series.

You never know where a lead is going to come from.

This second edition of *Opening the* Door contains two new stories and a section of shorter tales called "Short Sightings," which we began including in later volumes in our series.

At present, there are nine books in the *Sprits Between the Bays* series, two ghost books about haunted antiques, two volumes of beach oriented hauntings and other books about mid-Atlantic folklore and history.

I want to thank those who have contacted me, believing that I would do justice to their stories, and trusting that I would respect the desire of those who wished to remain anonymous.

I hope you will enjoy reading this revised version of *Opening the* Door.

Happy Hauntings, and don't forget to latch your door.

—Ed Okonowicz,
in Fair Hill, Maryland, at the
northern edge of the Delmarva Peninsula
—March 2003

The Bleeding Stone of White House Farm

The young girl was waiting in her room on the second floor of the farmhouse. It is not known whether she was a relative or a servant.

The hour was late, very late.

She heard the repeated sounds outside.

They weren't a surprise.

She had been awake and fully dressed, waiting under the bed sheets for him to arrive with their prearranged signal—the sound of a screeching owl four times in succession.

Her room was dark, like the rest of the house at two o'clock in the morning. One small canvas bag was packed with her few personal belongings.

Outside it was pitch black. The moon was hiding behind thick clouds. They couldn't have planned it better, she thought. It seemed even nature was cooperating, as if the gods approved of their decision.

The night they selected, that they both had been awaiting for weeks, had finally arrived. Within minutes she would leave behind her dull, uneventful world at White House Farm south of Kennedyville, ride through Chestertown and start a new life—far away and with him.

Nothing could stop them, now that their time had come.

All of the Isaac Perkins family, owners of the 600-acre farm-land and wooded estate, were asleep. Being about five miles north of Chestertown and with no neighbors nearby, the couple's only concern was that a stranger might pass along the road, and by chance look up the hill at the white farmhouse and notice them.

But there was little chance of that happening. It was a risk worth taking.

Slowly, she descended the back stairway, carefully avoiding the steps that tended to creak. The dogs knew her. She bent low and crept along the wide planked wooden floor. When she reached the animals she patted their heads. They yawned, gave her a bored look, and went back to sleep.

At the doorway, she turned, looked one last time at the Perkins home, where she had worked since she was a child. She cracked the door just enough to slip through the opening and entered the yard.

There was a slight chill. Just enough so you could see breath form a mist as it escaped from the mouth.

The girl stared into the black landscape.

He was there. She could see the faint outline of his body, under the largest tree and hidden by the wide trunk.

To her he was Prince Charming, atop his black horse waving for her to come. In his hands were the reins of the brown Chestnut he had brought for her.

She ran across the cold fall ground. But she didn't feel the damp frost. She embraced his leg and he pressed his hand against her dark hair.

They exchanged no words, afraid to utter a sound, lest they be discovered. Quickly, she mounted her getaway steed, secured her bag to the saddle and turned away from White House Farm.

They rode slowly at first, trying to be so very quiet, consciously holding back their excitement.

When they reached the edge of a steep slope, about 200 feet from the house, the girl kicked the horse with her heels, urging it to move faster—so they could begin their happily-ever-after life.

The Chestnut descended the hill at full gallop. The man urged his black stallion to follow, to catch up to his love.

When the girl's horse reached the bottom of the hill, it did not stop, but galloped on more quickly away from the house. It was simply following the signals and desires of its rider.

The man pressed faster to reach her, to pull along side, to slow her pace.

Then . . .

Within seconds it happened.

Their forever ended abruptly, as the girl's horse fell forward, stumbled and hit the ground at a highly dangerous speed. The bone in the horse's front leg snapped. The sound was unmistakable. It's leg had entered an unseen hole, probably dug by some animal. A hazzard that one would have been able to avoid in the daylight. But not in the ink-like blackness of the evening of their escape.

Her lover saw it happen, like it was occurring in slow-motion, right before his eyes.

His love, his bride to be, pitched forward, over the head of the horse that was falling toward the ground. Her hands let go of the reins. Her body flew through the air.

As her chest met the earth, she slid across the damp grass, moving forward until her head struck a single, exposed rock that was jutting out of the field.

Jumping from his horse, the man raced to his young love, picked up her limp body and held her face against his chest.

The girl made no sound. No mist of breath formed beneath her nose. No sound came from her lips. There was only stillness of the night.

The man took one final look at her face and carried away the horrible memory of a head covered with blood. His love was an unrecognizable creature who, only moments before, had been laughing and racing toward thousands of love-filled tomorrows.

As he gently placed her head back onto the blood drenched stone, the man let out a mournful cry that filled the farmland and forests of the Perkins estate, echoing into the darkness and awakening the creatures of the night.

In haste, and succumbing to the cruelties of *fate*, the man mounted his horse and rode off, his sight blinded by tears, his heart overflowing with pain.

They found her the next morning, with the injured horse nearby.

The young girl's smashed head resting against the blood-soaked rock, the only danger in the entire field. A solitary stone that should have been easier to avoid than to find.

The man never returned.

Some say, however, that she comes back.

Looking for him.

Seeking her love eternal.

And, until he is found, the stone continues to bleed—bleed with the bright red lifeblood of young love forever lost on that cold, fall evening more than 200 years ago.

No one will ever know whether the unfortunate events related to the legend of the Bleeding Stone happened exactly as suggested in that story. It is known, however, that the ghost of the unlucky young girl is only one of several spirits that visit, or have taken up residence, in White House Farm, according to long-time owner Kathryn Pinder.

She and her late husband, Arthur, bought the property, located on historic Maryland Route 213, in 1944, more than a half-century ago.

The legend of the bleeding stone was so well-known, Mrs. Pinder said, that when the state highway department changed the course of Route 213 several years ago—widening it and placing the new road in the path of where the stone was situated—the "Bleeding Stone" was moved from its original site to the top of the hill near the farmhouse.

"The bloodstained stone is in the rear yard," she said. "According to legend, a young girl eloping on horseback was thrown and killed when her head hit the large rock. It can be paint-ed or whitewashed," she added, "but the bloodstain will eventually reappear."

People stop by to see "the stone" often, she said. In 1992, her home was entered on the National Register of Historic Places, and its history and ghosts have been featured in books, newspaper articles and on Baltimore television programs.

Originally called the Ridgely Estate, the oldest section of the home was built by the Perkins family in the early 18th century. The date "1721" is visible on one end of the long, white farmhouse.

Records indicate that the mill on the property supplied flour to Washington's army while it was waiting out the winter at Valley Forge, Pa.

Colonel Isaac Perkins was described as a "Flaming Patriot." According to records in the state of Maryland archives, General Washington stopped at White House Farm occasionally while he was traveling on the old road that is now Maryland Route 213. In fact, Mrs. Pinder said, the nation's first president may well be one of the ghosts who sometimes visits the house.

Before moving into the French colonial-style farmhouse, the Pinders were painting the kitchen and heard footsteps coming from one of the rooms upstairs.

"I looked at my husband and he looked at me," Mrs. Pinder recalled, "and we thought it might be raccoons. We continued painting for about five minutes, but the footsteps continued as well.

"We didn't even turn the lights out. We left and came back the next day."

Unexplained sounds have occurred at different times during their stay in the home. One evening, about 10 to 15 years after they had moved in, Mrs. Pinder was awakened from her sleep. "I saw someone walking through the bedroom. She was wearing a blue nightgown and it looked like she was walking in a haze. The next morning, I asked my daughter what she was looking for in my room during the night. But she replied, 'I wasn't in your room.' "

That ghost never made a return appearance so Mrs. Pinder could not pursue the spirit's origins. But there were other mysterious tales related to the home that attracted the owner's attention.

Perhaps the most interesting ghost associated with White House Farm is the spirit of Mary Perkins Stuart, who inherited the family farm in 1768, when she was but a small child, upon the death of her father Thomas.

She died at age 39, on January 8, 1803.

Her grave rests beside that of her father, Thomas Perkins, in the family plot, that is located across the two-lane road and about a quarter-mile across the fields from the farmhouse.

The two tilted grave markers are worn, indicating their futile battle to hold back the effects of the elements. The overgrowth of the advancing wood line and downed trees make the gravesites difficult to find.

On Mary's gravestone, a long epitaph that reaches from tip to base, describes her as:

". . . pious, friendly and humane, amiable in disposition and as a wife and mother most affectionate, soothing and endearing perfectly sensible and resigned, the last breathings of her soul were "come Lord, let us come quickly. . . "

It's a well-known legend in Kent County, Md., that the ghost of Mary Stuart walks each year on the anniversary of her death.

Mrs. Pinder said that, until her husband's death in the early 1980s, they used to hold a grand party at White House Farm each year on the evening of Mary Stuart's death. About a half-hour before midnight, the guests were led across the cold, and at times snow- or ice-covered field, toward Mary's gravesite.

At midnight, all present would surround the tombstone, have a moment of silence and then Arthur Pinder would declare a verbal toast in Mary's honor.

(The liquid toast to Mary Stuart usually took place a little earlier in the evening, near the blazing fireplaces at White House Farm, Mrs. Pinder explained.)

Some of those present at the midnight gathering would walk over to Mary's gravestone and slowly run their fingers across a section of the curved, scalloped top, and make a wish.

"Many believe that wishes made in good faith at her grave will come true," Mrs. Pinder explained.

One night, immediately after the toast, the group heard the most unearthly sound from the woods.

"Someone said it was an owl. It was eerie that it occurred just at that moment. But, it could be something that just happened to occur by coincidence.

"We really were celebrating her life and observing it," Mrs. Pinder said. "I sometimes used to think, 'How many people are remembered in this way and for so long after they have died?' "

Reflecting on White House Farm, one gets a sense, a feeling, that Mary Perkins Stuart, George Washington, the unknown young

11

girl on horseback and the blue nightgowned phantom are still there, somewhere, in that state between where they ought to be and where they want to stay.

Those restless souls, and any other visiting spirits who happen to pass along the historic Kent County highway, would certainly find the French Colonial farmhouse—with its thick, 16-inch, brick walls, its wide, dark pine, random-width floor planks, the deep set window sills, old curved stairways and antique fireplace backings that had been shipped over from England—a hospitable haven.

Pennies from Heaven

Over a few cups of coffee late one night, Frank Terri's conversation turned to the topic of ghosts. Without a pause between steady sips of Joe and puffs of Camels, he was eager to comment on events associated with the spirit world.

"I'm sure there's something out there," he said. "Yeah! I would definitely say there's more to the spirit world, much more than people are aware of."

He said he has always believed in ghosts, and talked about them openly.

One of his earliest experiences occurred the night he saw his mother float through his bedroom. It was soon after she died. He swears he wasn't dreaming. But that was several decades ago, when he was only 15.

Years later, another incident occurred. Frank said he was close to his father-in-law, Tony, and the two men agreed that Tony would give Frank a sort of secret signal from the great beyond, after the older man died.

Frank said they arranged that Tony would return and tilt his framed picture, the one that hung on the wall in Frank's and his wife's bedroom. It was the two men's secret deal, and it would serve as a special sign for Frank alone.

"Yeah. Right after I got home from the funeral, I went upstairs, and there was Tony's picture. Hanging there tilted. I checked it before I left for the church, and it was fine. No way it could have been anything but a message from my father-in-law," Frank said, positively.

But, Frank admitted, his most interesting experience involving a relative who had passed away was also the most rewarding. It involved a contact from his older brother, Ben.

It happened only two weeks after Ben died. Despite the 19-year difference in their ages, the two brothers were very close.

"Ben was like a father to me," Frank said. "He was like an uncle, an older brother, everything all wrapped up in one. He was like the Godfather of the family. Now that he's gone, I'm the Godfather now," Frank added with a soft smile.

"It bothered me a lot that he was gone. I missed him. We'd go out together, eat together, go for walks together. It took a lot to get over him being gone."

The two of them used to joke about what would happen when one of them died. Ben always said he would come back.

"I laughed," Frank recalled, "and I said to him, 'If anything happens, I'll be in Atlantic City. Meet me there and give me a winner!' "

Two weeks after Ben died, Frank and his wife were at the Claridge Hotel and Casino, within view of the ocean and Boardwalk in Atlantic City. His wife tugged him on the shoulder and, pointing at a passing man, said, "Look. Doesn't that look like Ben?"

The man was large, like Frank's brother, and wearing a brown zippered jacket.

Frank nodded, but the sight of the stranger gave him an eerie feeling and he though briefly about Ben.

But he forced his brother from his mind and tried not to think about him. Later in the day, Frank was standing in front of a $1 slot machine on the upper floor of the casino. It was a machine that he and Ben had played together during an earlier trip to the Claridge.

Frank explained that Ben never liked to load the slots up. He tended to play one coin at a time rather than go for the big payoff.

"He wasn't greedy," Frank said, laughing, "and he used to snap at me about spending my money too fast."

It was in the evening and Frank changed a twenty for a roll of dollar tokens. He gave the cocktail waitress a one-dollar tip and had 19 slugs left.

When he was down to a single $1 token, he looked at the jackpot. Three 7's would give him $800.

Frank paused and started talking to his brother.

"I was whispering," Frank recalled. "I know it sounds corny, but I said, 'Ben. I know you're here. I'm going to put this last dollar in, and I'm going to turn my head.' Then I dropped it in and pulled the handle. And then the bells went off! And they kept ringing and wouldn't stop!

"I turned and saw three 7's there, and I said, 'Thank you, brother.' I know he was there, and he hit one for me."

Then, Frank paused, and gave a wide grin, "I've been asking him to come back and do it again, but he hasn't done a repeat . . . yet."

Old Blackie

It was in 1970, about five years after Al and Diane had been married when they rented an old, weathered, frame farmhouse, not too far from Selbyville, Del.

A truck driver, Al worked at odd times with a few days off and a bunch of days on. You could never really have any kind of a regular schedule when you were in that business. They wanted to find a house to rent, because apartment living had its drawbacks—too much noise from the neighbors walking around and coming and going all hours of the day and night.

They found a spot in the country, out near Hudson Crossroads, where it was quiet and peaceful. Not too much traffic, but within driving distance of shops and town.

The small two-story house had two bedrooms and a small storage area on the second floor. But the only bathroom was downstairs, along with the living room, dining room and kitchen.

They moved in during the winter, in January, and it was bitter cold. They decided to make one of the downstairs rooms into a bedroom, until spring. That way, Diane said, they could take their time painting the bedrooms. Since the top floor was unheated, they'd be more comfortable and warm through the winter.

Soon after they had moved in, Diane was home with the two children. Al was out on the road.

She kept a dimmer light on throughout the evening, so she could get up and take care of the children when they needed a drink or had to go to the bathroom.

"I woke up for some reason," she said, "and I saw a black figure move across the downstairs. It went from one room to the next, floating like. I remember it was shaped like a monk with a hood and hunched over, like it was wearing a black shroud.

"It may sound silly, but I remember thinking if he sees me looking at him, maybe he'll bother me. So I'll just peek and then he'll go away. The next morning I tried to tell myself it was my imagination."

Diane didn't tell Al about the black monk when he returned home, but she did mention the racket coming from the second floor.

"I would hear noises, like something was moving big pieces of furniture up there during the night," Diane recalled. "It seemed to be coming from the attic area that was off to the side of the upstairs, an older area that was built above the kitchen. I told Al to go and put some D-Con up there, but he told me he had done that before we moved in."

Later, when spring came, they moved upstairs into the front bedroom and Diane started hearing laughter. It sounded like a woman's voice, and it occurred both during the day and night. It, too, seemed to be coming from the storage area.

"I'm not the kind of person to be afraid," she said, referring to her work as a medic with several area volunteer fire company emergency care units and a lot of experience camping with her family while growing up.

"I specifically didn't tell my husband, because I thought he'd think I was going crazy."

Toward their first fall, before they had completed a full year in the farmhouse, Al and Diane were reading in the bedroom that was entered by the stairs that led directly from the kitchen.

They had secured the wooden stairway door with a hook and eye, to keep it open so heat would travel freely up the staircase.

Just as Al shut the light and his head it the pillow, he heard an unusual sound and immediately jabbed Diane with his elbow.

"Do you hear that?" he whispered.

She nodded, indicating that she did notice the sound of footsteps that were walking slowly up the stairs, heading directly to their bedroom entranceway.

Al slid his hand under the mattress and pulled out his pistol.

They both moved off the bed and crouched behind the side that was farthest from the doorway.

The steps got louder. . . closer.

They kept advancing at the same slow, steady pace.

Al pulled back the hammer of the .38 caliber revolver, ready to unload the chamber into the intruder.

Then . . . just as they estimated from the sound and number of footsteps that the unwelcome visitor should be standing in the bedroom entrance, there was . . . .

Nothing.

No figure.

No more sounds.

No target to shoot at.

In the stillness and the dark, Al and Diane tried not to breath.

Then, the footsteps resumed, except they were moving away. Down the staircase. Toward the kitchen. Getting softer as the distance increased.

"But what was so odd," she said, "was when it got to the bottom of the stairway, it closed the door completely. We had the door kept open with a hook and eye. That thing, whatever it was, must have undone the hook, and then it actually shut the door.

"It took about 10 days for us to move out. We told the land-lord we needed a bigger place, because the children needed more room. He was a nice man and we didn't want to tell him his house was too spooky for us to live in."

Al and Diane moved about a half-mile down the road. Over a period of the next eight years, they noticed that the next several renters never stayed too long, only a few months at the most.

"The house sat empty more than it was rented," Diane recalled. Word in the area was that the landlord's mother had lived there alone for a long time and she had died in the house.

In the safety of their new home, Al finally admitted that he, too, had seen the black, monk-like figure roving the downstairs. But, he said, all that was behind them now.

In 1980, almost 10 years since they had left the haunted house, Diane was working in a convenience store in Fenwick Island, Del. It was a hot, thick, humid August afternoon and she thanked the Lord for having the good fortune to work in an air-conditioned setting.

A young woman came into the store, bought a soda and asked if she could hang out and soak up the free AC.

"I said sure. But, now," said Diane, pausing to explain the chance encounter exactly as it happened, "this next part of what happened really scared me to death and made my hair stand up on end."

The woman, whom Diane had never seen before, said, "I didn't get much sleep last night. My son kept me awake."

"Is he teething or sick?" Diane asked.

"No," the woman said, giggling, "our spook was moving furniture around all night."

"What are you talking about?" Diane asked her.

"The place we live in has got spooks," the girl said. "And the bad part of it is, when I went downstairs to get him a drink of water, there was Blackie floating through the living room."

A chill went through Diane's body. "Where do you live?" she almost shouted, forcing herself to try to remain calm.

"In an old frame house out near Hudson Crossroads."

Diane was in shock. "How do you live there? We used to live there years ago!"

The girl finished her soda, then laughed as she walked out the door, "As long as they leave me alone, I'll be all right. But they better not bother my son."

"When I got off work," Diane said, "I rushed into the house and told my husband. He stared at me. Was real still for a minute, then he said, 'I think I'm going to be sick.' "

Diane continued. "I remember the girl looking at me. I must have turned white. I never talked to her again, never saw her again. I think her name was Kristin. I have to tell you, it still sends chills up my back. But it does confirm what we saw and that we weren't crazy."

Unexpected Cellmate

The tiny peninsula formed where the Little Elk Creek and the Big Elk Creek meet southwest of Elkton is an interesting geographical and historical site. The land near the convergence of the two streams attracted the attention of the Cecil County, Md., government when it decided to build a new detention center on the marshy wetlands in the early 1980s.

Others, however, believed the location had been a popular site for centuries. A group of area archaeologists arranged to make exploratory digs, before construction began, to determine if the long-held belief that an Indian village had been located there was correct.

When members of the Northeast Chapter of the Archaeological Society of Maryland and staff of Mid-Atlantic Archaeological Research did excavations on the 13-acre site, what they found was interesting. Their efforts uncovered hundreds of pieces of American Indian pottery, more than 100 arrowheads, and, about four feet below the surface, a skeleton in a grave.

The human bones were sent to the Smithsonian Institute, which returned a report dating the remains to be from about 1,400 A.D. Encouraged by their success, the archeological team continued its efforts and found more gravesites. Their locations were logged in, noted and left undisturbed.

Their exploration, however, verified that the small peninsula had been the site of a large Indian village and burial ground. The convergence of the two creeks was an attractive site. Even hundreds of years ago it was recognized as being a good location to establish a settlement, for it was easier than other open spaces to defend, and the water routes encouraged accessibility and trade.

Years later, in the early 1800s, the area was the site of Fort Hollingsworth, which served as both a trading post for settlers and a military outpost for the Maryland militia.

After the archaeological procedures were completed and documentation recorded, construction began.

In the summer of 1984, the Cecil County Detention Center, operated by the Cecil County Sheriff's Office, was officially opened. It was common knowledge that the prison was built in the vicinity of an Indian burial ground. In fact, for some time, there was a display in the main wing of the new building of arrowheads and Indian tools and pottery found in the area.

In the last few months before the prison was ready to accept its first occupants, correctional staff were assigned to stay overnight to maintain security and keep the curious away.

Jane, who has worked for the sheriff's office since it was housed in the Old Jail on North Street, heard stories from night shift workers who said they were bothered by unexplained footsteps, saw lights go on and off and heard howling sounds that seemed to be rushing through the halls of the empty center.

It was during the early days at the new facility, when the prison population was well below its 128-person capacity, that Jane learned of a very unusual experience.

With only about 85 prisoners, each inmate was able to have his own four- by eight-foot cell. Mike, a small time criminal who was serving time for a light offense, was assigned to out-of-cell duty cleaning offices.

"This guy was no wimp," Jane said, thinking back on the incident. "He was in his mid 20s, used to associate with bikers, and he was a big guy, 6 foot and 200 pounds. He came into the office and looked scared. I said, 'What's wrong, Mike?' "

He looked around, she said, as if he wanted to make sure no one could hear him. "You're not going to believe this," he told Jane, and then went on to explain.

After the usual 11 p.m. lockdown the night before, Mike said he fell asleep and was awakened in the wee hours of the morning. While his eyes adjusted to the dark, he noticed that he couldn't move his arms. They were pinned down, tight against his body, by the hands of an Indian chief who was straddling the prisoner's body and pressing down hard against him.

"Mike said the Indian was wearing a bonnet full of feathers and war paint," Jane said. "He tried to move and wrestled with the spirit, and said he ended up struggling with the ghost for most of the night, until daylight. He said there never was any talk between them. But he was really afraid, to the point that he asked to be moved into a different cell with another guy. He said he felt better at night with someone else around."

Jane said Mike never saw the Indian again, and no one else admitted to seeing the warrior either.

"It was so real to him," she said. "When people say, 'He looks like he's seen a ghost!' that was the case, here. He was so pale and it was obvious that he had a rough night. It was hard, really something, for him to admit what happened. He wasn't the kind that wanted anybody to think he was afraid. I don't think he ever went into that cell again. It didn't bother him to walk by it during the day, but at night, he wouldn't go near it."

23

Not far from the prison

Oldfield Point Road runs southwest from Elkton and parallels the Elk River. Until recently, it was a quiet, unnoticed area of the county, a bit off the beaten path—visited by boat people in the summer and the year-round residents who lived in small cottages by the water's edge.

Now, passers-by can see pockets of development, as more and more commuters discover the scenic setting and the calming, picturesque views of the nearby Elk River.

But what rests nearby or even beneath some of the newer properties is questionable. Residents of certain homes in the areas off Oldfield Point Road have reported seeing circles of fire and hearing chanting in the late evenings.

No logical explanation has been found.

Rumors and hearsay, however, suggest that the answer may be that some homesites are located uncomfortably close to more undiscovered old Indian burial grounds.

Who is alive to tell?

How is one to know, for sure?

Secrets of the Barn

T he small hamlet of Conowingo, Maryland, is located not far
from the Pennsylvania border and hugs the rocky banks of
the mighty Susquehanna River. Travelers passing through
the area along old Route 1 can sense the age of the settlement
from the appearance of the rolling farms and historic homes built
of attractive, colorful stone.

Many of the buildings were constructed hundreds of years
ago. Like places everywhere, some structures have been well kept
and bear their age proudly. Others seem to be hanging on, waiting
to be rescued and resurrected to their former glory or razed and
put out of their misery.

The appearance of the land in that northernmost sector of
Cecil County, with its deep valleys and rocky landscape, is dramatically different from the flatness of the rest of the Eastern Shore.

For slaves secretly heading toward freedom during the Civil
War, the change in the scenery and presence of hills was an indica-
tion that they were close to the Mason-Dixon line, the symbolic
border that separated the Free State from the Keystone State, the
South from the North. Nearly 130 years ago, that border crossing
was the goal of those seeking freedom.

In the 1970s, a contractor bought a farmhouse located on one
of the winding country roads north of old Route 1. One of his first

projects was to build a three-room apartment in the basement. The owner decided the basement rooms would be ideal for his children. His plan was to redo the entire building, literally, starting from the ground up.

Soon after settlement, the large barn that also was located on his newly acquired property collapsed to the ground. As he and his crew began to sift through the rubble, the owner decided that the 150-year-old, weathered barn paneling—with its attractive silver patina—would be ideal for the walls of the farmhouse's recently renovated basement bedrooms.

Soon after the weathered siding was installed, unusual events began to occur.

The family's French poodle, which initially had been content in the new homestead, refused to descend the farmhouse stairs and enter the basement rooms.

Unexplained sounds were heard, especially after dark.

While raking leaves in the yard one afternoon, the contractor turned and noticed an old Amish man standing nearby. The bearded stranger in dark clothes and a straw hat was helping with the fall chore. As the new owner took a few steps in the man's direction, and began to call out a greeting, the unexpected helper, the Amish man, he . . . just . . . disappeared.

But the family became concerned with the seriousness of the unexplained occurrences when a metal cross, placed on the newly paneled wall in the basement, flew off the wood, traveled across the room and landed on the floor at the opposite end of the room.

Desperate and concerned, the owners contacted a Delaware medium, who agreed to hold a seance in the farmhouse.

When she arrived, the psychic took a cross, which she wore around her neck, and hung the gold chain on a nail protruding from the paneling.

Immediately, the nail bent downward and the cross and chain fell to the floor.

When evening arrived, the psychic and several of her students gathered in the haunted farmhouse basement, under a dim light that added to the serious mood of the silent setting.

A black woman, who was a member of the medium's group, announced that she had made contact with two disturbed spirits. Several others who were present at the session saw the hazy spirits of a pair of young black men appear in the room.

In the midst of the seance they focused on the black woman, to whom they cried out, pleading, "Help me!"

The clues to the solution of the mystery came in segments. Messages were relayed silently to several in the medium's group, who shared them with the others.

When the isolated statements and incidents were interpreted, the following explanation was developed:

Because of its proximity to Pennsylvania, in the late 1850s the large Conowingo plantation had been one of the final stations on the Underground Railway. Originally, an Amish man had owned the property and he and his family helped the slaves reach freedom by offering them shelter and then guiding them across the nearby Mason-Dixon Line.

When the Amish farmer died, the property was sold to a man who did exactly the opposite. He held the slaves for his own use and also took many south and sold them back into slavery.

After holding two slaves who were brothers for some time, he took them outside, had them stand against the side of his barn and, without warning, shot them. As they fell to the ground, their blood splattered on the wooden walls behind them.

Apparently, the shooting happened so fast that the two lost souls didn't realize they were supposed to be dead. The spirits of the restless slaves mingled with the barn paneling where they were shot. Then the ghosts moved into the farmhouse when the silver wooden planks were erected in the basement.

The medium was able to communicate with the spirits of the two dead men. She convinced them to rest in peace by leading them through the open psychic door, which she closed behind them as they passed.

As she walked up from the basement, the psychic and the relieved family members noticed the immediate change in attitude of the small French poodle. It cheerfully ran down the stairs toward the new rooms for the first time in months.

Buyer Beware

J oy and Johnny Ray were sitting in their living room. They have three children, and all of them walked in and out during the lengthy conversation. There was no effort to lower voices to a whisper or hide what was going on from them. They had heard it all many times before. In fact, two of them had lived through several of the experiences that were being discussed.

Johnny Ray works as a mechanic. Joy is a homemaker.

It was late morning. The sun was shining. A normal day in a three-bedroom apartment just east of Newark, Del.

After brief introductions, the conversation turned to the subject of our gathering—the family's ghost. More correctly, their former ghost.

It happened 10 years ago. They said the memories were still fresh, because they, or anyone else who has lived through something like this, will never forget what happened.

The couple had been looking for a way to get out of apartment living for months, but with no luck. Houses were too expensive to buy, and renting a home wasn't much cheaper. While scanning the classifieds one morning, Joy noticed an offer to take over the outstanding payments on a mobile home. After getting the basic facts and directions, she and Johnny Ray drove out to take a look.

There were only a half-dozen other trailers in the small community, so it was easy to find. It was a good sized mobile home,

29

about 70 feet long with two baths, three bedrooms, a living room and large eat-in kitchen. It also had a large wooden work shed, located right outside the kitchen door.

Even though it was located below the C & D Canal—in southern New Castle County, Del., within sight of the Maryland border—it wasn't too far for Johnny Ray to drive to work.

During their conversation, the agent casually asked if it bothered Joy and Johnny Ray that someone had died in the trailer. They looked at each other, said nothing for a few seconds, then smiled, shrugged their shoulders, and said, "No."

Excited and pleased, they gave a deposit and agreed to assume the mortgage payments. Soon afterwards, they moved from their cramped apartment with their two small children. It was fall, the weather was mild and the scenery was beautiful.

Exhausted from hauling boxes and belongings, the family decided to throw a mattress in the living room and sleep on the floor the first night.

"I remember I just couldn't get to sleep," Johnny Ray said. "In the middle of the night, I opened my eyes, looked up, and saw the face of Abraham Lincoln looking at me through one of the livin' room windows. I didn't know anything, but, later, a neighbor told my wife that the guy who had lived there before us looked just like Abraham Lincoln."

"That's right," Joy added. "They said his kids used to ask, 'Why is Daddy's head on a penny?' The resemblance was that close."

It wasn't long before the footsteps started. Then the whistling. Having the lights occasionally flickering on and off was another annoyance they couldn't ignore.

Outside, in the shed that was built by the previous owner, the lights would turn on by themselves, late at night. Often, when that happened, they would burn into the early morning, then go off just before sunrise.

The neighbors noticed it, too.

The shed was big, said Johnny Ray, large enough for a small Volkswagen to fit inside. You could only enter it through a heavy sliding door. Its windows opened from the inside with a crank. The door was secured with an oversized padlock.

The light switch was inside, but there was another one inside the trailer. The former owner had wired the place himself.

"I always checked," said Johnny Ray, "before I went to sleep, that the lights in the shed were off. And nobody touched that switch in the middle of the night. The neighbors, they said it was Bobby, that was his name. He was just out there a workin' in his shed for a couple of hours. He loved to tinker out there, they said, 'til all hours of the mornin'. So they figured his ghost had came back and took up where he'd left off."

A few months after they had moved in, during late winter, Joy was reading the morning paper. She almost screamed when she saw a small article in the local news section.

"I recognized our address, in one of the police reports," she said, "about . . . about a murder!"

The newspaper account referred to the shooting of Bobby by his girlfriend in the master bedroom of their trailer, the same place where Joy and Johnny Ray now lived . . . and slept each night.

She ran outside and confronted the first neighbor she could find.

"They confirmed it," Joy said. "All the neighbors knew about it. But no one wanted to scare us. We found out the man was shot in the back of the head by his girlfriend a few months before. She killed him because she found a motel receipt in his pocket. She shot him in the head while he was asleep.

"Then," Joy added, "they say she put the gun to her head, pulled the trigger, and shot herself in the temple. Gave herself a lobotomy. She lived and is in jail somewhere. They say she has no memory and is blind, from the shooting."

The apartment was silent.

I looked at Johnny Ray, who seemed to read my mind as he answered my next unspoken question.

"It was a little creepy, all right," he said, nodding, "but we decided we'd just have to deal with it. At first, nothin' happened, other than the small stuff we mentioned. But it explained the face I saw of Abraham Lincoln, in the window that first night."

But other things happened that grabbed the family's attention and gave them the impression they had gotten a few more unexpected extras thrown in when they bought the property.

One day, Joy noticed a red stain on the carpeting in the master bedroom.

"It was dark and looked like a bloodstain, under the edge of the bed," she said. "I'd clean it up until there was nothing, and then, a couple of weeks later, it would come back. That kept happening for a long time."

But the tiny spots on the mirror were worse.

There were tall, flat mirrors attached to the front of the pair of sliding closet doors in the master bedroom. Joy walked by one day and noticed a group of tiny rust colored speckles. She shot them with a spray cleaner and they got brighter. She realized the dark dots looked like dried blood.

"I'd keep cleaning them and they'd keep coming back, sometimes the next day, sometimes a few weeks later," she said. "It went on the whole time we were there, all three years. Holly, our daughter, who was about 10 at the time, would bring her friends over to see the bloodstains and they would all freak out."

"My wife scrubbed and scrubbed and the spots kept comin' back again and again," Johnny Ray said.

He added that blood showed up in the edges of the door jamb and on the inside of the master bedroom door, which also served as a rear entrance and exit from the mobile home.

"It was the way they took him out, after he was shot," Johnny Ray said. "There was blood on the door. We started at the top, with hot water and a sponge," he recalled, "and tried to clean it goin' downwards. It was bright red, like somebody saturated the whole thing with blood.

"It was like an Alfred Hitchcock movie, and I remember thinking, 'Oh, Man! *This is something!*' So much flowed, it was like the door was bleeding. It was a real creep out."

"I don't think it was supernatural. It was just creepy," Joy said. "We weren't really afraid. And our ghost wasn't mean. But he did pick on my husband a bit."

Johnny Ray shook his head as he recalled the Friday afternoon he had arrived home from work. He was exhausted and handed his pay over to Joy, who was heading out to the grocery store. He said he planned to take a nap while she was gone.

"I was really wore out, went to the kitchen, got a beer and flopped in bed," Johnny Ray said. "No sooner did I hit the mattress, when the bed moved all the way from one side of the room and then flew back to the other side. All by itself. It was like a force just picked it up and pushed it one way and another.

"It was a heavy, queen size bed, made of pecan, with heavy covers on it. I couldn't sleep in there, so I just got up and went and sat in the living room."

But there were other things besides the phantom footsteps and late nights at work in the shed.

"You could hear him breathin' from time to time," Johnny Ray said, "feel it as he was passin' right beside you. It was heavy breathin', real thick. And I'd keep hearin' him whistlin' the same tune all the time, over and over."

Eventually, they adjusted to the spirit's continuing stream of surprises.

"We had to make jokes to make it through," said Joy. "We'd say, 'Bobby's mad about something,' or 'Bobby's at it again,' or 'What's wrong with Bobby, today?' "

"We had to make a joke to sort of lighten the situation," agreed Johnny Ray, "to make the best of it."

But they didn't stay forever.

It was the breakdown of the mechanical systems and appliances that finally made them decide to leave. The stove wouldn't operate properly, the freezer in the refrigerator broke down. The heater wouldn't work right and the electrical and mechanical systems in the mobile home also started to malfunction.

Joy said one of her girlfriends knew a medium who came to the mobile home. The psychic tried talk to the ghost and told Bobby it was all right to go on.

"The woman said she took Bobby home with her, to her home in New Castle, but I'm not so sure," said Joy.

After more than three years of unforgettable experiences and a collection of spooky stories they could use to entertain their friends, Joy and Johnny Ray sold the mobile home and moved back upstate . . . into a dull, uninhabited, spirit-free apartment.

And the trailer?

"It's downstate somewhere now," said Johnny Ray. "I don't care where it is, as long as it's not here. But," he paused, and softly added with a smirk that comes from being a safe distance away, "I still hear stories that it's still not right."

Unlucky "9"

F or centuries, the shoreline of the Delaware River has played
an important role in the progress and development of the
region. Since ancient times, Indians hunted and fished
along its banks. When the first settlers arrived by sea, they used the
small watertowns as centers for both trade and transportation.

In more modern times, large ships, their bowels bulging with
crude oil, arrive daily at the refineries that press against the
water's edge. Transporting and transferring millions of gallons of
flammable cargo is an unglamorous, dirty and dangerous business. It's a trade carried out by specialists, blue collar workers who
are rarely recognized, or thought of, until tragedy strikes.

Workers' deaths from explosions and accidents with heavy
machinery have occurred. And others have been killed while they
were fighting industrial fires and trying to rescue the injured.

In the midst of black and gray shadows, restless, uneasy spirits not only roam the Colonial mansions and the weather worn
cemeteries of the peninsula. Secretive specters also are found
among the storage tanks of dirty refineries and in the darkest corners of crumbling warehouses in abandoned industrial sites along
the Delaware River.

❖   ❖   ❖

It was midnight.

The dark time when most people are asleep.

For those on the graveyard shift, there will be no closed eyes until the sun starts to appear. These workers are the sentinels of the darkness, the keepers of the flame. While we rest, they keep work-sites secure, make sure energy continues to flow and maintain idle machinery, so daylight workers can shift into full-force production when they arrive each morning.

Tony, a young bachelor in his early thirties, was alone that spring night. But that wasn't unusual, he worked by himself a lot. It was what some would call a perfect evening: No clouds, lots of stars. There was no breeze at all. The air was totally still, so you could hear the smallest sounds from the farthest distance. The faint smell of oil hung in the air, just enough so you could notice it was there.

Tony liked the solitude of the dark. The quiet gave him time to think, reflect on the past and plan for his future. In particular, he focused on what kind of job he would get when he finished his math degree. He was attending classes part-time at nearby Neumann College in Aston, Pa., close to where he lived.

He was a third generation oil refinery worker. Some said he had black oil in his veins. It ran in the family. His father, and his father's father, had worked in the 100-year old site, just north of the Delaware-Pennsylvania line, about halfway between Wilmington and Philly.

He was an operator, a guy who made sure that the millions of gallons of crude moved smoothly and safely through the refinery's miles of pipelines .

"I had a strange feeling that night," Tony recalled. "Something told me that something out of the ordinary was going to happen to me."

He was walking through the rail yard area. There were nine sections—spotting areas where the big Conrail tank cars were loaded with fuel oil. Each section was about 100 yards long and 50 yards wide. They were numbered 1 through 9, and each of the areas was marked with a huge, white metal sign bearing the individual number, in black, of the different sections.

"I left a small building and then cut through an area that was off the beaten path," Tony said. "I looked up, and I saw the number 9 start to move, like it was painted on a pendulum. It was swinging back and forth, about one-third of the way, from, say, four to eight o'clock on the face of a clock.

"I stopped. I was scared to approach any closer. Then, the whole thing started spinning all around, like a wheel at the carnival. It scared me to new heights. I mean, here was a piece of metal, with a black number 9, attached to a metal post. It had been there forever. And it was spinning around and around."

Tony walked backwards, his heavy workboots stumbling against the dark, steel railroad tracks. He wanted to get to a more familiar place to regroup. . . to gather his thoughts and figure out what he saw, what was happening.

"As I left the area," he recalled, "I saw an energy, a glowing force go right by. It was, maybe, 15 yards in front of me. It's hard to explain, but it was like a light with a form. It wasn't vaporous. It was like a glowing mist.

"I fled the area and headed into a nearby shelter, a place where I used to work. It took me about 20 seconds to get there, and as I was walking, the glow moved from side to side."

As if to stress that he wasn't crazy, Tony said he is pretty open minded about the unexplained, and he considers himself a bit more receptive or prone to see things like he experienced that night.

"Sometimes, I know what people are

going to say before they talk," he said. "I'm a hard working guy with a 3.7 index at college. I'm not crazy. But I can believe there are things out there, in the refinery, because of the many ill-timed deaths that have occurred here. We lose lives because of the nature of the business."

He said the refinery process is dangerous. Men have been killed in on-the-job accidents, burned, crushed, fallen off the docks and disappeared. There also have been instances when ships have exploded nearby, or in the refinery's docks, and the bodies were thrown into the river.

"All I can do is tell you what I saw," he said. "There's no way a 9 should be out there spinning around on a perfectly still night. I tried to approach the area afterwards, but I just couldn't get near that 9 area for a few days. The experience really terrified me. It really shook me up.

"I was afraid to a talk about it. Not just because I might experience ridicule, but I was emotionally affected. I'll never forget it.

"One interesting thing, though, I knew something was up that night before the 9 started spinning. I couldn't have imagined that happening. But a few minutes previously, I caught myself looking over my shoulder. I had a feeling somebody was watching me."

Weeks after the incident, Tony was talking to an older worker, a black man who had been at the refinery for several decades and had worked in every corner of the two-square-mile complex.

"He looked a me, with a very serious expression," Tony recalled, "and he said that, years ago, there was an area in another part of the refinery where they would always send him and another younger guy to work together. It wasn't anything they could explain, but it was because of a feeling they had. He said he was just plain scared whenever he went over to that section.

"As best I can figure," Tony added, "that same feeling manifested itself to me on that spring night. I'm a perfectly stable individual, and I know what I saw. And I'll never, ever, forget it."

Mist and the Moving Broom

B arbara is a school teacher. Now in her mid 40s, she lives alone in a house near the Nanticoke Indian Reservation lands east of Millsboro, Del., moving there from Pennsylvania about 10 years ago.

But, apparently, she doesn't live alone.

"From the end of my bedroom," Barbara said, "I can hear muffled sounds down the hallway. It sounds like there's a small crowd, like a bunch of people are talking. It gets loud enough to get annoying. But when I walk into the room, it suddenly stops."

One afternoon, when a girlfriend was visiting, she asked Barbara, "What's that noise? I can hear what sounds like a crowd of people talking."

"After a few minutes," Barbara said, "it disappeared and everything was all right."

There's also the unexplained smell of cigar smoke that materializes for no apparent reason.

"I don't smoke, and no one who comes in here does, because I can't stand smoke. But it's there, the smell of cigars from out of nowhere. I'm sure that sooner or later I'm going to run into something else, something bigger. I can just feel it."

Barbara's instincts are based on many years of personal, unforgettable, unexplained experiences. She has witnessed strange events her entire life. They started when she was young and surfaced dramatically when she was a teenager, growing up in Chester County, Pa.

Smiling as she reflected on her past, Barbara said the current voices at the end of the hall are tame compared to what happened many years ago.

At 17, she was living with Norma and Gary, a young married couple, in a stone farmhouse that was more than 200 years old near the Delaware-Pennsylvania border.

After moving in, she noticed a decorative, straw broom leaning against the wall, on one side of the stone fireplace that was located in the oldest section of the house.

Eventually, the straw broom began to move, from one side of the fireplace to the other and, at times, across the room. No one who lived there could explain why or how the broom got to different sections of the room.

One day when Gary questioned why the broom was being moved so much, Barbara said, "I know I put it back where it was. Somebody, or something, must be moving it."

"Sure," he said, sarcastically, "it must be a ghost."

Barbara and Norma smiled as he said it.

"We all laughed and even gave him a name. We called our ghost Oscar."

Whenever phantom footsteps occurred they seemed to come from the upstairs rooms in the oldest section of the house. These two bedrooms—one of which was Barbara's—were located directly above the fireplace.

In the black darkness of one early morning, Barbara was awakened by a sound that she could only describe as "a ball of paper being dragged along and rubbed against the wall."

"I awoke," she said, "and I saw a mist or a fog. And the more I stared, the more it took shape. Eventually, it appeared to be a man with a wide brim hat. There was something else over his shoulder, but I couldn't make it out. Then, he started to stare at me, right at me. It really frightened me, and I put the covers over my head and tried to ignore it, to hide. When I got up to go to school, I told Norma and Gary. They told me it was just my imagination."

A short time later, Gary's mother—who was in her 60s—was coming to stay in the farmhouse for a few weeks.

"Don't tell her anything about Oscar," Norma told Barbara. So they all made it a point to avoid any mention that the home might have a resident spook.

"Gary's mother was staying in the other bed in my room," Barbara said. "The first night she was there, I heard the sound of the paper rubbing against the wall again. I didn't want to look, so I closed my eyes.

"Suddenly, I heard Gary's mother talking to someone. I looked up over the covers and there was no one else in the room. But Gary's mother was talking. Then she turned on the light and told me what she saw.

"The next morning when she explained it to Norma, she too realized it was exactly what I had seen before, except that Gary's mother said she saw a woman's form, with long blond hair, taking shape behind the man's—Oscar's—figure."

Other people who visited the home sensed there was someone else there.

When Barbara was dropped off from a date one evening, she and her boyfriend saw "Oscar" waiting for her under a tree near the driveway.

"I remember running into the house," Barbara said. "I would run up the stairs, close my eyes and never look at anything. I remember saying, aloud, 'Please. You know I'm afraid of you. Please don't let me see you.' I bought a bracelet in the Pennsylvania Dutch country with a hex sign and an arrow on it. When I went to bed, I used to have it on the stand and grab it and hold it all night. I grabbed it that night, for sure."

She wasn't the only one scared

"At first, my date got white as a ghost," she recalled. "Later, he said that Gary was outside, dressed up like Oscar, trying to scare him. But I told him it was the real ghost, Oscar himself, in his big black hat. I knew both Norma and Gary were in bed when I came in. They both called out to me and asked if I had a nice evening."

On another occasion, while some friends were in the basement, they saw Oscar's reflection in an old mirror and ran over each other trying to get up the narrow stairs.

During the last few days that Gary's mother was at the home, the older woman was seated alone on the front porch. Later she said she heard a voice behind her whispering either "Wait. Don't rush," or "Rush. Don't wait."

Barbara said the older woman couldn't remember which of the two messages she heard. But a few days later, Gary's mother was rushed to the hospital.

As Gary, Norma and Barbara were driving to the hospital for a visit, Norma said she had just smelled the heaviest, overpowering scent of flowers in the hallway before they left. She said it was like she was attending a funeral.

Later that day, Gary's mother died.

"It was like some messenger was trying to tell Gary's mother, on the porch, what was going to happen, to be patient," Barbara said.

Strange incidents continued in that home. Barbara said she even got to the point of tying the moving broom to the metal fireplace shovel and poker with heavy string in several double knots. Still, it would somehow get loose and be found in another area, and her knots were still tight and untied.

"We all moved out about two years later," Barbara recalled, "and no one else moved into the home. I used to drive by from time to time to see what was happening. The land was sold, and there was supposed to be a shopping center built on that site. But before the house was knocked down, it caught on fire.

"Even though it was supposed to be abandoned, I heard that the firemen said they heard someone screaming inside the house. They tried to get in, but couldn't. Afterwards, they checked but couldn't find a sign that anyone had been there.

"Living there was an experience. Later, I got interested in ghost stories and I was reading an article in a newspaper. It described a form taking shape from a mist or fog and turning into a person, the same way it happened to me in the upstairs bedroom. I always knew I wasn't imagining it, but reading that helped.

"Over the years I've learned to deal with this sort of thing. I really don't care whether people believe me or not. I know what I saw. I tried to figure out everything that happened, to come up with a logical explanation. I even tried not to believe it.

"In the end, what I've found is that there are a lot more people who believe in the unexplained than there are those who don't believe."

The Residents of Woodburn

Woodburn, one of Dover, Delaware's, most popular tourist attractions, was built in 1790 by Charles Hillyard III. The nine-room, brick Georgian home in the center of the First State's historic capital city was owned by Hillyard descendants until 1817, when it was purchased by the Cowgill family, who kept the property for 95 years.

It was during the Civil War era when Daniel Cowgill, a Quaker, dug a tunnel connecting the mansion's cellar to the banks of the St. Jones River, allowing escaping Southern slaves to secretly enter Cowgill House and use it as a stop on the Underground Railway. (While that tunnel passageway has been sealed, the thick, heavy wooden door still remains across what used to be the hidden entrance into the mansion's cellar.)

Daniel Hastings bought the home in 1912, but sold it in 1918 to Dr. and Mrs. Frank Sullivan Hall, who filled Woodburn with fine antiques.

Over the years, the structure and its surrounding gardens also have been referred to as Woodburne, Woodbourne, Hillyard Hall, Cowgill House and Woodburn Hall.

In 1965, it was purchased by the state of Delaware for $65,000, and became the official residence of Delaware's governors. To date, seven chief executives have occupied the home:

Governor	Term
Gov. Charles L. Terry Jr.	(1965-1969)
Gov. Russell W. Peterson	(1969-1973)
Gov. Sherman W. Tribbitt	(1973-1977)
Gov. Pierre S. du Pont IV	(1977-1985)
Gov. Michael N. Castle	(1985-1993)
Gov. Thomas R. Carper	(1993-2001)
Gov. Ruth Ann Minner	(2001-present)

Approximately 5,000 visitors tour the first-floor public areas of the governor's home each year. They leave impressed by the detailed construction of the historic brick building—with its Dutch-style entrance door, tall windows, large rooms, wide pine staircase, handmade interior paneling and fireplace wall cupboards—plus the fine collection of 19th-century furnishings, antiques and original period paintings.

But there are other unusual, unseen and unnoticed features of Woodburn that most visitors, tourists and guests do not see. These entities have been present in the mansion for hundreds of years, and their stories have been passed on through whispered gossip, oral folktales and local legends. More recently, they have been the subject of research, investigations and newspaper and magazine articles.

They are the ghosts of Woodburn—and they have been present long before the late Gov. Charles L. Terry Jr. spent his first night in Delaware's premiere haunted executive mansion.

Even today, the ancient phantoms of the night still cause superstitious adults to cross to the opposite side of the street. And passers-by can see school children break into a run as they approach the stately Georgian mansion on Kings Highway.

When the state was considering the purchase of Woodburn, the late Bill Frank, well-known Delaware journalist, wrote several stories about the Dover home, and included a number of details about its legends and ghosts. Frank expressed positive opinions about the state's need for a governor's mansion and, in one of his "Frankly Speaking" columns, wrote: "Woodburn is a beautiful house. If it is available for $65,000, more or less, it's a bargain and somehow should be preserved as a public building—ghosts and all."

At least four spirits are reported to haunt Woodburn. Over the years, however, different versions of each ghostly inhabitant's tale have surfaced and been related by various tellers and authors.

In a magazine article in 1966, the wife of the late Gov. Terry was quoted as saying, "So you've heard about our ghosts. . . . It's such fun to live in a place that's distinguished enough to have legends. In England every house worth its history has a ghost or two."

It's obvious that from the very beginning of its reign as Delaware's premier home, the possibility of phantoms on the prowl in the governor's house has been viewed with a sense of status, as a tradition to be displayed proudly rather than kept hidden in the building's Colonial-era closets.

In keeping with that fine First State ghostly tradition, the following stories offer a summary of the spirits who are believed to reside in the official home of Delaware's governors.

The Colonel

The first ghost reported to appear in Woodburn was nicknamed "The Colonel," and he was seen as early as 1805. The most often told incident occurred while the home was owned by Dr. Martin W. Bates and Mary Hillyard Bates.

But the ghost was not seen at that time by the owners. Instead, it was encountered by Lorenzo Dow, a Methodist evangelist, who was conducting several revivals in the Dover area and was a house guest of the Bates family during his stay in the region.

According to several published sources—including a written recollection by Judge George Purnell Fisher—the minister was descending the stairs on the second floor on his way to breakfast. On that early morning, he encountered a gentleman clad in the interesting dress of the preceding generation—including knee breeches, pigtailed hair and a ruffled shirt.

Minister Dow reportedly smiled and nodded at the stranger, assuming he was a recently arrived relative or guest. At the breakfast table, Minister Dow was asked to lead the family in grace. In response, he asked if those gathered should not wait for the "old gentleman" he had met upstairs.

The heavy silence that descended upon those at the table was broken when Mrs. Bates answered, quite shortly and emphatically, "There is no other guest in this house!"

Minister Dow said grace and received evasive replies from Mrs. Bates when he tried to describe and discuss the "old gentleman" he had encountered on the stairs. However, before he left the house, Mrs. Bates told the minister, in confidence, that she also has seen the "old gentleman." She asked Minister Dow not to share the incident with others, for, she added, according to his description, the spirit on the stairs was that of her father, Charles Hillyard. He had died several years before while living in Woodburn.

It is said Minister Dow was never invited back to Woodburn. But, apparently, he must have shared his ghostly experience with someone.

There are, however, other versions of the ghost called "The Colonel." One legend suggests that a Continental Army officer died at Woodburn soon after the Revolutionary War, while the mansion was serving as a veterans' hospital. It may be this wounded warrior's spirit that haunts the stairs and hallways of the governor's home.

While the home was rented to the Fisher family in the late 1800s, young George Fisher brought a friend home from school to spend the Christmas holidays.

The guest was given the room once occupied by the long deceased builder Charles Hillyard. But as soon as the friend had been left alone, young George Fisher heard a scream from the direction of the guest's room.

The young host and his father found their young guest in a lifeless mound on the floor. When he was revived, the young man said when he opened the door he saw a man seated beside the fireplace. But it did not remain there. The specter got up and started to walk toward him, causing the young guest to faint.

Records do not note where the young guest spent the rest of his evenings while staying in Woodburn, or if he decided to pass the balance of the days of his vacation elsewhere.

The room often referred to as the "Ghost Room" is now used as the master bedroom on Woodburn's second floor, directly above the great front door.

One guest, who stayed in that room during the time it was owned by the Hall family (from 1918-1953), was awakened three times during the night to get up and relock the door. When he awoke in the morning, he found the door unlocked, wide open and his glasses broken.

There is one interesting note about Charles Hillyard III, Woodburn's builder and first resident, who Delaware author George Alfred Townsend wrote, was "a tyrannical, eccentric man. . . .

"The owner, it was said, amused himself by making his own children stand on their toes, switching their feet with a whip when they dropped upon their soles with pain and fatigue. His own son finally shot at him through the great northern door with a rifle or pistol, leaving its mark to this day to be seen by a small panel set in the original pine."

The shooting story has two versions. The other, shared in the book *Recollections of Dover in* 1824 by Judge George Purnell Fisher, who had lived for a time in Woodburn.

The judge's document states that old Mr. Hillyard was in a fit of rage and passion directed toward one of his sons. While chasing the boy with pistol in hand, the irate father is said to have fired the weapon just as the boy was running out the north—main entrance—door of the home. The written account by Fisher states that the "son saved his bacon by slamming the door to and the ball entered the door."

Today, the top section of the Dutch-style entrance door, while painted over many times, still bears the raised mark where filling has been applied to cover the entry spot of either Mr. Hillyard's pistol ball or his son's rifle shot. (Depending, of course, upon which version you believe.)

The Slave Kidnapper

Amongst the landscaped grounds of Woodburn are rows of shaped English boxwoods, evenly lined hedges, scattered crepe myrtles and several tall pines. Until 1999, when it was cut down for saftey concerns, a tall tulip poplar towered above other trees in the mansion's backyard. Its thick branches reached out like fingers of a gnarled hand toward the sky. At its wide base, the dark trunk was split, revealing hollows large enough for a man to stand inside.

On foggy nights, some say, you could see the ghost of a dead man hanging from the tree, rusty chains still grasped in his hands, rattling in the wind.

Much of this well-known and often repeated Kent County legend is based on the chapter entitled "The Cowgill House" in *The Entailed Hat* by George Alfred Townsend.

According to that author, Patty Cannon of Johnson's Crossroads near Reliance—the notorious murderess, thief and gang leader, who stole free and escaping slaves and sold them back into captivity—raided Woodburn to kidnap a group of slaves who were gathered in the basement.

When officials and Quaker owner Daniel Cowgill chased off the raiders, one would be slavenapper hid in the branches and hollows of the large tulip poplar. Unfortunately, the fellow lost his hold and fell from his hiding place in the center of the tree. But the descending body never reached the ground, for the man's neck was caught between two intertwined limbs. It was there that the unlucky slave robber was strangled by the gnarled poplar's thick branches.

Some still refer to the tall tree, that stood in the governor's yard, as "The Hanging Tree." And that ghost is said to moan and rattle chains in that phantom tree and in the cellar, near the tunnel entrance where the slaves were huddled during the raid.

A different version suggests a slave who was trying to escape a band of pursuers hid in the trunk of the tree, but was captured. Still another tale says the moans are the cries of slaves who were captured or killed in Woodburn.

The Tippling Ghost

It is often recalled that the late Gov. Charles L. Terry Jr., the first official occupant of the state's executive mansion, said he would engage in conversation with the "tippling ghost," a "wino" who enjoyed visiting the wine storage area of the cellar and draining the bottles.

Prior owner Dr. Frank Hall is said to also have had experiences with this particular spirit who enjoyed his "spirits." The former Woodburn resident would purposely fill decanters to the brim with fresh juice of the barley in the evening, and the "tippling ghost" would empty the bottle by morning light.

According to Terry, one Woodburn servant swore that he actually saw a ghost relaxing in the dining room, slowing sipping a glass of wine. The servant described the specter as an older man, wearing a powered wig and dressed in Colonial era garb.

It's been suggested that the visitor may be the specter of the original resident, Charles Hillyard, who was known to enjoy a drink or two in his day.

The Girl in Gingham

The last of the primary group of ghosts is the small child dressed in an old-fashioned, red gingham dress and bonnet who has been seen in the formal gardens, by the reflecting pool, located to the side of the house.

One report is that she carries a candle around the brick walkway near the pool. Since the reflecting pool was placed on the property while Woodburn was owned by Del. U.S. Sen. Daniel Hastings (from 1912-1918), the small girl is probably one of the mansion's most modern specters.

Gov. Terry claimed that the child would sometimes come into the kitchen and sneak a drink of wine.

More Recent Events

Sande Warren Price, a member of Gov. Thomas Carper's staff and an employee of the State of Delaware's Division of Facilities Management, served as Woodburn's general administrator.

She was responsible for the coordination, scheduling and overall supervision of the state building. She also has heard, and, to a degree, experienced some unusual activities.

When her son, "Drew," was four months old, she brought him to Woodburn and placed him in a battery-powered swing in her second floor office, just off the building's back staircase.

She was working downstairs in the kitchen, but could hear the swing and her son's sounds through the receiver from the baby monitor that rested on the kitchen counter.

"The swing, moving back and forth," said Price, "sounded like a washing machine. Suddenly, the sound stopped dead."

Worried, she and a co-worker ran up the stairs to see her son, sitting quietly in the silent, unmoving swing, his eyes staring directly across the room at some unseen figure or object.

51

"And," Price added, "the swing switch had been turned off. It wasn't that the batteries died out.

"The swing was actually turned off. And no one was there who could have done it," she stressed.

It is in a guest room on the third floor of the mansion, Price said, that a short, five-foot-high door, leading to a small storage area, refuses to remain closed. At times, the bed covers on one of the beds is disturbed and the throw rugs moved or turned over.

During Halloween, Dan the Van Man, a WDSD disc jockey, stayed in the room overnight while performing a remote broadcast.

"But," Price said, with a smile, "he played it safe by pushing the headboard of the bed against the door, to keep it from opening."

One group of employees who spend a lot of time, much of it alone, in Woodburn are officers of the Capitol Police Department, who are responsible for round-the-clock security.

Several have witnessed or heard of unusual events in the Governor's Mansion, and some admit they are less than eager to spend time there alone, especially in the evenings. They have heard footsteps, doors opening and closing and other unsettling sounds during both the day and evening shifts.

Some officers pass time in the control room during their shifts playing the card game Solitaire. But, when they have left the desk area to check out a sound, or make periodic rounds, they have returned to find the neatly, lined-up cards of their uncompleted game tossed together in one large, jumbled mess.

Officer Greg Spielman had worked at Woodburn for several years. He said that he had never believed in ghosts—until he heard stories from fellow officers who had worked for many years in Woodburn and in other area museums.

Spielman remembered the evening he heard footsteps and the sounds of doors opening and closing. He said he investigated the noises several times. During each check, he made it a point to shut the kitchen door. But every time he responded to an additional noise, he noticed that the kitchen door, that he had firmly closed, was open.

After investigating the disturbances several times, he was unable to discover any evidence of an earthly or unearthly presence. But the experiences were real, he said, and they were enough to make him more than slightly uneasy.

A bit frustrated, he noticed that the clock indicated that it was after midnight. While returning to the building command post, Spielman said he called out aloud to whichever of the Woodburn spirits might be active that night, "You were here before I was here, and you'll be here after I'm gone. You've got the run of the place, just don't break anything!"

Information for the details and background of this story was obtained through personal interviews and from appropriate material included in books and periodicals featuring the history and ghosts of Woodburn.

These sources include:

Woodburn: The Governor's House of Delaware by Emily N. Hart

National Directory of Haunted Places by Dennis William Hauck

The Entailed Hat by George Alfred Townsend

The Haunting of America by Jean Anderson

Sunday Bulletin Magazine

The Baltimore American

Sunday News Journal

Allentown Evening Chronicle

Wilmington Morning News

National Enquirer

Saturday Evening Post

Philadelphia Inquirer

Elizabeth

Smyrna, Delaware—founded in 1768—is a pass through town, a small treasure of rural America that people go by rather than visit. For years, beach traffic heading south toward the Delaware shore and resorts hardly noticed the residential and small business districts to the west of Route 13.

In 1994, with the opening of Delaware Route 1 relief route, which allows travelers to speed even more quickly toward their downstate destinations, Smyrna has become even more isolated and overlooked.

But, those who turn off the busy highway traffic and enter the Colonial-era town are rewarded with a view of the winding streets, stately trees, irregular brick sidewalks, ornate Victorian houses and stately Federal-era homes.

On quiet evenings, when the roundness of the yellow moon shines through the craggy branches of 200-year-old trees, one can imagine the people who have called the little town "home." But some souls, perhaps, have lingered a bit longer than is customary and are not in any great hurry to move on.

On West Mt. Vernon Street—an old and narrow thoroughfare in use since the days of horses and carriages—stands the "Cloak House of Arts." It was constructed around 1791 and currently is owned by Ruth Knotts, who named it after the Cloak family, the original builders and long-time residents.

Ebenezer Cloak, the earliest member of the prominent family, was an associate of President George Washington, who recognized Ebenezer for his contribution to the Revolutionary War by outfitting a privateer.

From the late 18th century, until the early 20th century, the home—which was enlarged and given a Victorian-style appearance in the 19th century—was the residence of descendants of the original owners. The family, who were well known architects became related, through marriage, to at least two of Delaware's earliest governors.

It wasn't until 1931 that the home was sold to a close friend and passed out of the direct line of Cloak descendants. In 1967, Ruth Johnson Knotts and her late husband, Donald, purchased the home and, in the 1980s, named it the "Cloak House of Arts," where Ruth and several teachers gave music lessons.

"The Cloak family lived here for so many years," said Ruth, who was seated in the oldest wing of the home on a sunny fall afternoon. The large, formal parlor—able to comfortably accommodate her grand piano—has a high ceiling, tall windows, built-in wall shelving and two brick fireplaces.

"It's about the only house in the area that had been inhabited by the family that had built it, and for so many generations," Ruth said.

She pulled out detailed records of the property, explaining that the original land grant came directly from William Penn to William Green in the 1680s. Photographs of members of the Cloak family were collected during her research. She displays them with a sense of reverence and a degree of familiarity, referring to some of the deceased Cloak descendant's interests, hobbies and marriages.

It was soon after Ruth and her late husband moved into the home that they seemed to sense there was someone else in the building. The couple lived on the first floor and turned the second and third levels into apartments. But there were footsteps on the second floor when it was vacant. They also heard someone talking. Mr. Knotts passed away in 1975, and Ruth continued giving a piano lessons in her home.

"I would hear footsteps," Ruth recalled, "and the sound of singing . . . singing by someone with a very soft voice."

In the mid 1980s, a mother of one of Ruth's students was seated in the hall, waiting for the youngster's session to finish.

"I came out into the hall, and the woman asked, 'Do you have a ghost?'

"I said, 'I think it is quite possible.' The woman said someone came beside her and, in a wee, soft voice, whispered, 'Hello.' The mother said she smiled, very calmly, and looked around. But no one was there. She said she was sure she felt the presence of a ghost, but she wasn't afraid and it wasn't scary."

A more dramatic event occurred to a painter Ruth had employed to brighten up the third floor apartment. She described him as a "big, lumbering, macho man, in his early 40s."

Ruth was working on the first floor and he came barreling down the steps, heading for the safety of the first floor like the top of the house was on fire.

Running to Ruth, he asked, "Who's up there? Why didn't you tell me you had a ghost?"

"Why? What happened?" Ruth asked.

"She slapped me across the back of my neck a couple of times! And I wasn't doing anything but painting!"

Ruth smiled, recalling the incident, saying her painter refused to go back up to the third floor that day and left in a huff, more insulted than scared, she added.

"But he came back and finished the job. He still comes back to do odd jobs," she said. "Every time he comes, he asks, 'Where is she?' I can understand her not liking him. He's forceful, and she didn't like him up there, in her private space."

Ruth laughed, saying the ghost seemed to move up to the third floor to get away from all of the music lessons.

About six years ago, two tenants who had lived in Florida took a lease on the third floor apartment. Two days after moving in, the wife approached Ruth asking if there is a ghost in the building.

The new tenant said things were being moved in the apartment and that her husband was laughing at her for thinking it might be some sort of spirit.

Smiling, Ruth told the woman, "She will not bother you. She's not mean."

Thinking back on the experience, Ruth said, "I don't know why I always called the ghost a 'she.' I didn't know it was a woman, and I didn't know her name.

"But I wasn't surprised about the tenant's comment," Ruth continued. "People wouldn't be up there any more than a day or two when someone would come and ask: 'Do you have a ghost?' "

This particular tenant told Ruth that a candy dish she had placed in the kitchen had been moved into their bedroom. When she asked her husband if he had done it, the man said, "I not only didn't move it, I haven't been eating any of it."

"Well, it must have been the ghost," the wife said, picking up the dish and carrying it in two hands as she walked across the room.

As the husband laughed at her explanation, some unseen and unexpected force hit the underside base of the dish, causing it to leap out of the wife's hands, scattering candy across the floor of the apartment.

A few months following that incident, and a few days after Ruth had received a letter and photograph from one of the Cloak family descendants who was living in Florida, the wife from the third floor apartment visited Ruth.

Noticing an old picture, featuring three women posing on the front porch of the Cloak home in the early 1900s, the tenant said, "Oh! That's the ghost!"

The woman could give no reason for her statement, for neither she—nor Ruth—had ever seen the spirit resident of the home. But the tenant made the comment impulsively, automatically, as if she couldn't control herself.

Interestingly, Ruth recalled that a few days earlier, she had stared at the same photo and said to herself, *"There's my ghost. Elizabeth."*

"I don't know why I even thought that," Ruth recalled. But, the fact that she knew the identification of names written on the back of the picture were incorrect and the unsolicited announcement by her tenant allowed her to feel comfortable in finally naming the Cloak house ghost.

Further research and a conversations with a local historian indicated that Elizabeth Cloak Wilds was one of the last family residents in the home. She, apparently, was a creative person who loved music, other people and parties. However, her energetic nature was possibly confined by a restrictive husband.

Elizabeth, the daughter of Ebenezer and Cristiania Cloak, was born in 1850 and died in 1918.

"I have never seen her," Ruth said, thinking about her long-time house guest. "Would I want to? I wouldn't mind. There's a sort of benevolence here. I think she wants to safeguard things. She wants to be here to watch over things and make sure the house is okay."

When Ruth was preparing to go on vacation for a week, a number of unexpected and irritating things kept happening at home that caused her to delay her trip for several days.

She had placed a load of clothes in the dryer on t.
porch and went to do some work on one of the upper flc

"Suddenly, somebody kept saying to me, '*Come down.*
look around.' I went down and I could hear a woman's voice,   ...i-
ing to me in my mind. It was like someone saying: '*Go to the door!*' It
was a prodding presence, an uneasy feeling. As I opened the basement door, I smelled smoke. I went down and saw a soft, burning
glow in the circuit breaker box. It was on fire.

"If I had not been there that day, and if it had not been for
Elizabeth, I wouldn't be here in this home now. We caught it in time.

"I just talked to her out loud, and said, 'Thank you, Elizabeth!
I really appreciate that.'

"I really feel that the things that held me up from going on
vacation at the original time I picked were to keep me here,
because the house would have burnt down if no one was home."

In 1992, Karen, Elizabeth's great-great-great granddaughter,
visited Ruth. The two women stayed up into the wee hours of the
morning, talking about the house, history, the Cloak family . . . and
about Elizabeth.

It was soon after that visit that the presence of Elizabeth
seemed to disappear, Ruth said.

"I have a feeling she was satisfied in seeing her great-great-
great granddaughter. And Elizabeth wanted you to know she was
here, but she never showed herself. I think she was trying to say:
'*I'm here. I want you to know I'm here, and I belong here*' "

Ruth doesn't know if Elizabeth left with Karen, or if she just
moved on to her final place of eternal rest.

"I've had a feeling she was pretty much possessive of the
house, in a nice way, until she would find out who lives here and
what they are going to do," Ruth said.

Perhaps, Elizabeth's work is done, and she is happy having
seen her family members. She also may be very satisfied that the
historic Cloak family home, nestled in the center of quiet Smyrna,
is in very good and caring hands.

59

Golden Mine Farm

On Williamsville Road, across from Blairs Pond a few miles south of Milford, stands Golden Mine Farm. Originally, the property was an 800-acre tract of farmland and mills that also took in the area around nearby Griffith Lake. Today, about 100 acres of that plot is still owned by descendants of the Colonial-era owners.

The original farmhouse was built in the mid 1700s—before the American Revolution—and it has witnessed the passing of travelers, workers and visitors for more than 200 years.

Janet Kennedy, who now owns the property, lives in the modern brick home that is separated from the original homestead by a low, green tenant house.

Standing in front of the original farmhouse, Janet pointed to the door of the building that is covered with weathered cypress shingles. That entrance, she explained, opens into the small room that had been used as overnight lodging by circuit preachers when they traveled the villages of Delmarva on horseback. It includes a fireplace and has space enough for a small bed.

At the opposite end of the building—the wing with exposed brick—there is a dark, metal plaque that proclaims the structure as being listed on the National Register of Historic Properties recognized by the United States Department of the Interior.

The three front doors and five windows on the building's sides, said Janet, indicated to those at the time it was built that the owners were people of influence and financial means.

Located in the side yard, at the base of a towering tulip popular, are several weathered tombstones. Some standing, others leaning and broken, their carved and etched markers indicate the remnants of the family graveyard, the final resting place of many of the property's owners and ancestors.

Perhaps, Janet said, the family gravesite is related to some of the unexplained events that have occurred in and near the original cypress and brick farmhouse.

It was in that building's dining room that her brother, Robert, who had lived in the farmhouse at one time, noticed that during parties and on other occasions the lights in the dining room would sometimes flicker and dim.

"We thought it might just be bad wiring," Janet said, "after all, it is an old place."

Later, Robert bought a number of antiques from a shop in Smyrna. Among the people who made the delivery was an older woman, in her 70s and of European birth. She walked into the farmhouse, went straight to Robert and told him there was a good, spiritual presence in the house.

For the last dozen years, the home has been occupied by Cynthia Oliver and her husband, Karl. They moved in on Halloween Day 1982.

A registered nurse, Cynthia said she has seen the same ghost about six times. It always has occurred outside, during daylight, near the dining room end of the original front section of the farmhouse.

The first sighting took place about mid day, a few months after the Olivers moved in. Cynthia had picked up the mail and was walking on the driveway, toward the side entrance of the house.

On the porch, in front of the door that leads to the dining room, was a woman, standing as if she was waiting to be let into the home.

Cynthia described the figure as young—in her 30s—with a long black mourning dress that went from her neck to her ankles. The figure also wore a small white cap, appearing Amish or Shaker in style, that didn't cover all her hair. Her hands were clasped at the waist.

She had very dark hair, but very fair skin, said Cynthia.

"She was not a solid, human body," Cynthia recalled, "but the form was enough so that you could see she was a person. She was very pretty, kind of striking. My reaction was I looked, stopped and stared for a few seconds and she was gone. I was a little startled. I didn't think a whole lot about it. I kept it to myself for a while and didn't tell my husband."

Cynthia explained that a sister and aunt have had unusual encounters, so the experience wasn't anything she had never heard of before. When she did tell her husband, his reaction was skeptical, and, she added, it was treated like a family joke for some time.

Over the next several years, return appearances of the woman in black occurred without warning, but always during daylight. Several happened in early morning when Cynthia was out in the front yard.

"I'm always outside when I see her, and she is standing on the porch or at the base of the steps. Generally, I've seen her from the side. After a while, all of the instances kind of blend together. because they are so similar."

It might be that one other member of the Oliver family has seen the woman in black. When Cynthia's son was three years old and able to talk, they were playing on the side of the house, near the dining room.

Cynthia recalled the event. "He looked at the porch and said, 'Who's that?' He said it to me. He didn't say 'What's that?' He said 'Who's that?' There was no one else around, so his attention was not directed at anything or anyone else."

A few years after experiencing several incidents, Cynthia was conversing with neighbor Janet Kennedy, her brother, Robert, and their mother, Virginia Simpson Kennedy.

When Cynthia described the ghost, Robert—who used to live in the same historic house—said he got a cold chill. He explained there always seemed to be something odd going on in the dining room. He added that his children even gave the ghost a name. They called her "Millicent."

As the conversation continued, and Cynthia described the ghostly woman in black in more detail, Janet's mother Virginia said the description led the elder Kennedy to believe the image might be her grandmother, when the descendant was young.

Later, Virginia sent Cynthia a family picture to examine. The result was both eerie and amazing.

"It was the person I'd seen!" said Cynthia. Her hands were folded, as they were when she was waiting at the door. I used to think I was imagining it, but I was relieved when I saw this picture."

The photograph was of Mary Ann Griffith, Janet Kennedy's great-great-grandmother—born April 14, 1844, died August 15, 1870—the last person know to be buried in the small family cemetery.

Some think that Mary Ann Griffith died during childbirth, at the age of 26, in the room where Cynthia now sleeps. There is another interesting connection between Mary Ann and Cynthia. They were born on the same day, "April 14," but 110 years apart.

Ask Cynthia what it all means, why she was selected to be able to see the ghost and she offers a few explanations.

"I wonder if she might be our guardian angel," Cynthia said. When her son was 18 months old and had just been moved from his crib to a bed, Cynthia was awakened by a voice shouting: "*Get in there!*"

When she arrived in her child's room, Cynthia was able to reach her son just as his head was about to hit the floor.

"I have a feeling that sometimes spirits present themselves to people who will be receptive to them. I feel her presence at times. I don't feel threatened in any way. I'm not afraid of her and it's not unsettling.

"I get the impression that she's waiting outside, looking at the door, hoping for someone to let her in. Usually, when I see her, I'm close enough to call to her. But I've never really tried to contact her in that way. I intend to get a copy of her picture and put it in the dining room, as a tribute to her."

Apparently, her husband has had a change in attitude.

"I think he believes what I'm talking about, now," Cynthia said, smiling. "One day Karl was outside walking around and I asked him what he was doing. He said, 'I'm waiting for her to come.'

"I smiled and said to him, 'It doesn't happen that way.' "

Mary Ann Griffith

Image from a photograph provided by Virginia Simpson Kennedy

Skinny Hands and the Gypsy

I t's said common traits can be found in persons who belong to the same family—brothers and sisters who may act alike, and children who carry on a talent or interest of an older relative.

These characteristics may be good or bad, depending upon one's opinion. They can be intelligence, dumbness, creativity, frugality, laziness, artistic abilities, criminal behavior, cruelty and good old-fashioned determination, to name just a few.

If so, sensitivity to what most consider the unseen and the unexplained may be a trait shared by both Eydie and her sister, Hannah, both of whom reside in Ocean Pines, Maryland.

Eydie

When Eydie was a youngster, growing up in Washington, D.C., she would make up ghost stories and tell them to her friends on summer evenings and eerie nights around Halloween.

She smiles as she remembers how much fun they all had, and how much she enjoyed being the teller of mysterious tales.

"I would scare them, and I'd scare myself," she recalled. "All of the kids were afraid to get into bed. I told this one story about 'Skinny Hands.' They were connected to long, skinny, bony elbows that came up from underneath the bed, and we all were afraid that they would grab us in the darkness. It got to the point where I was so scared that I would run into the room and jump into bed."

Today, in her spacious Ocean Pines home near Berlin, Maryland, the retiree talks rather calmly about a lifetime of encounters with the unusual and the unexplained.

In 1945, while living in New Jersey, Eydie awoke in the early morning light, but didn't want to get out of bed. After a few extra moments of relaxation, she felt a force, a sense of steady pressure, surrounding her head and pressing against it from all directions. She described it as if someone was trying to crush her skull, but by using a pillow.

Years later, while Eydie was living in Glen Burnie, Maryland, the experience occurred again. This time, however, it also felt as if someone or something unseen was trying to pull her out of her bed.

"It was not a dream!" she stressed. "I was conscious and I knew I was awake. I was being pulled. And not just my head, but my whole body, was being squeezed."

On another occasion, while resting in bed she felt immense pressure, as if a large, black cloak was being drawn over her.

"It was cold and dark and evil," Eydie recalled. "It was nothing that I saw. It was just what I felt. I was also being squeezed and I was trying to get away. It only lasted a short time."

Eydie said these incidents only occurred when she was tired and attempting to rest, not while she was up and about or wide awake.

"I have no explanation," she said, "but I thought it might be that the devil was trying to enter or possess me. Eventually, I began to talk to whatever it was and say, 'Okay! Do your thing, right now!' "

After consulting an acquaintance who was knowledgeable in the occult, Eydie was warned not to antagonize or challenge the unknown spirit. Instead, she was instructed to burn a solid blue candle.

"For a time that worked," she said. "But then things started up again."

She was awakened one night thinking that the gentle feet of a small animal—about the size of a cat—were stepping around her head, leaving soft impressions on her pillow. But, Eydie realized as this was occurring, she had locked her bedroom door.

To be sure of this, she stepped out of bed and looked throughout the room.

There was no cat anywhere.

As soon as she returned into bed, placed her head on the pillow and closed her eyes, the catlike footsteps pranced again.

There also was a snapping sound, as if someone was pulling on sheets of aluminum foil near her face. This was accompanied by a breeze, like a piece of paper was being waved back and forth across her head.

"The minute I opened my eyes, it stopped," she said, "and the minute I closed my eyes it started again."

Her children offered "logical" explanations, such as mental lapses, exhaustion, imagination and vivid dreams. But Eydie stressed that she was awake, did not imagine these things and discounted the helpful suggestions of others to easily explain the complexities of the unexplained.

On at least two occasions, she explained that she had heard the sounds of a group of airplanes, as if they were revving up their engines before takeoff, just before two unusual events occurred. When it happened while in Ocean Pines, her husband said he did not hear the airplanes, but Eydie said the engine sounds were distinct, recognizable and very loud.

In her present home in Ocean Pines, things she owned—such as pages of sheet music, recording tapes and a cloth—have disappeared, while other items that she did not own have appeared.

After wiping her kitchen counters with a wet dishrag, Eydie tossed it into the sink. But, within seconds, she saw another spot that needed to be wiped. When she looked in the sink to pick up the recently used cloth, it was gone. It had totally disappeared.

Eydie also discovered a folded up $5 bill on the floor in the center of a room.

"I said, 'Thank you!' to the poltergeist, or whatever, and placed it into my wallet," Eydie said, with a smile.

Later she found the thick broken base of a glass Coca Cola bottle in her kitchen. (She only uses plastic soda bottles.)

While trying to toast two slices of bread one morning, Eydie placed an empty plate on the counter beside her toaster. Immediately, the plate moved, on its own, about three feet to the left and stopped at the opposite end of the counter.

Eydie calmly picked up the dish and checked to see if its base was wet, or if there was a pool of liquid standing on the counter that might have caused the dish to slide.

The countertop was dry. She placed the dish down in its original position, and the plate slid away a second time.

Eydie grabbed it in both hands and pressed it hard against the top of the counter. This time, it stayed in that position, and she had her toast.

On a Sunday morning, when her children were young, she fell into bed and noticed she was looking at her feet . . . . The base of the bed was slowly, but very definitely, being lifted into the air.

"I remember saying, 'Don't tell me this is happening to me.' "

Thinking it might be her two sons, who were under the bed lifting the base of the furniture to scare her, she jumped out of bed and looked underneath the mattress.

There was no one there.

But as soon as she got back into her bed, the raising of the bed's base started up again.

"When you tell people about these things," Eydie said, "most of them look at you like you have two heads. But this is true. If people tell me that things happen to them, and it hasn't happened to me, I believe them. Why shouldn't I?"

One evening in their home in Ocean Pines, with her husband asleep in bed beside her, Eydie had just closed her eyes and felt a small little hand resting in the palm of her outstretched hand.

"I jerked my hand away and called to my husband, 'Tom! Tom! There was a hand in my hand!' But he just ignored it. I wouldn't put my hand out again. It was small, like a child's hand."

While reflecting on that strange event, Eydie was quiet a few moments, then offered a possible explanation.

"When I felt that little hand in mine that one night," she said, "I thought about 'Skinny Hands,' the story I used to tell when I was young, even though the hand that night wasn't skinny, just small." Then, after pausing, Eydie added, "I've never really been afraid of all this. But I won't get out of bed without turning the lights on."

Hannah

It was years ago, while she was living in an apartment in District Heights, outside Washington, D.C., that Eydie's sister, Hannah, saw a ghostly figure sitting on the edge of her bed.

"He was a most handsome pirate, extremely dashing," Hannah said, recalling the event with a noticeable sense of excitement. "He had a white blouse with large sleeves, an earring, and a there was a bandanna around his head. No beard.

"I knew him. I hadn't seen him for ages, but we had a conversation. He talked to me, through my mind, and I answered him aloud. He stayed about five minutes."

Hannah said her son came into the room and asked her to whom she was talking. But she explained that she was only reading to herself.

Later that day, Angelina, a gypsy friend called Hannah on the phone and said, "You had a visitor, a pirate, there today! He was not allowed to come. He was not given permission to come and see you."

Hannah was amazed that her friend knew what had occurred, for Hannah had told no one. But, she would later discover, the gypsy knew more than Hannah could try to imagine.

A few years later, Hannah had gotten the feeling there was a ghost in her home. She had a sense of not being alone and noticed that things were being moved about.

When Hannah's daughter-in-law was visiting, the younger woman said she had seen a Spanish looking woman, about 5' 5" tall with very dark hair, walking in one of the bedrooms. She was very disturbed about it.

Hannah made a telephone call to Angelina. The gypsy calmly described the Spanish woman, without seeing her, and she also told Hannah the ghost's name was Barbara.

Several months later, Hannah's daughter-in-law had lost an earring and the two women searched the entire apartment and could not find it. At midnight, when the two women were sitting on a couch in the living room, the earring dropped out of the air near the ceiling and landed on the carpet between Hannah and her daughter-in-law.

Hannah calmly looked up and said, "Thank you, Barbara, for finding the earring. We appreciate it."

It was while Hannah and her husband were taking a trip across the country that another incident occurred. They had stopped on the side of the road to rest while driving through Tennessee.

Hannah said something told her to open the car door. She did, and a cat moved through a nearby field and walked out of the bushes toward her. They let the animal into the car and took it with them into their motel room.

"It was strange looking," Hannah recalled. "There was something unusual about it. We got it something to eat, but it didn't wash its face like other cats did. It sat on the bureau and was just staring, watching me."

Hannah had decided to take the cat home with her. But, when she awakened the next morning, the animal was gone. She searched the room, but it had disappeared. No one had let it out. No one had opened the motel room door. It was a mystery they couldn't solve.

A month later, when Hannah had returned home, she got a phone call from Angelina. The gypsy said, "I'm glad you didn't take that cat, the one that you had in the motel, with you. It was evil."

"I hadn't said a word to her," Hannah recalled. "There was no way she could have known about the cat and what happened on the trip."

Luther

The year was 1969. Barbara had just moved into a very old 10-room Cecil County farmhouse. The building still stands where it has for more than 100 years, a fair distance off the main road that leads from Newark, Del., to Rising Sun, Md.

The old, white stucco section of the building was large, with several doors that led out onto the wide, wrap-around porch. Out back and off to both sides were several outbuildings—a large wooden hay barn, a few weathered tool sheds, a milk house, and a number of garage and work buildings where the machinery was kept each night after a hard day working the several-hundred-acre plot.

Her children were small then. Cassandra was 7, Katie only 2 and little Arthur, who was named after his father, had just celebrated his first birthday.

They lived there for 25 years, until the summer of 1994. That's when Barbara left. Most of the children had grown and moved out a few years earlier. She decided it was too big for one person, and she couldn't keep up the place by herself. She moved into an apartment with Cassandra. But Barbara admitted being just a little sad that she had to leave Luther behind.

That's what she named him.

Luther.

Barbara still doesn't know why she picked that name from all of the many ones that she knew. It just came to her, flew into her mind, and she blurted it out.

"Luther."

It seemed to fit, though. The rest of the family agreed that it was a perfect name for a ghost, their very own ghost for a quarter of a century.

The house had seven bedrooms, two downstairs and five upstairs. Two stairways led up to the spooky, low-ceiling attic. Like most houses a few hundred years old, it was built in sections. Under the original, front section was the cellar, with stone walls, a dirt floor. It was quite a bit smaller than the rest of the house.

Off to one side of the old wooden stairs that led into the dark, damp underground room was an old freezer. In the opposite corner, on the left, was a small rectangular box.

"It was just sitting there," recalled Katie, who now works as a cosmetologist. "It looked like a little, child-size, white coffin."

Barbara remembered it being there when they moved in. You couldn't help notice it every time you went down to the cellar to use the freezer, she said.

Being the oldest, Cassandra, now an X-ray technician, said she would be sent into the cellar to place food in the freezer.

"I would throw the stuff into the freezer and run up the stairs," Cassandra recalled. "When mom said the freezer had burned out "it was the happiest day of my life. 'YES!' I shouted."

At that point, about five years after they had moved in, there was no longer any reason to go down there. Barbara said everyone, even her husband, felt uncomfortable about the cellar. So they nailed up the basement door that led from the first floor and then pushed a heavy piece of furniture in front of the doorway.

"No one ever opened that cellar door or that little coffin," said Katie. "But I knew we would find a box of bones in there."

And no one liked to be alone in the farmhouse.

Only a week after moving in, everyone had gone out on errands except Barbara's husband, who was in the shower. He heard the windows of the house rattling and the doors banging and slamming shut. When the family returned, he was in a nervous state and told them never to leave him alone in the house ever again.

"It wasn't long that we were there that I knew we had a ghost," said Barbara.

"It started with the walking—a step, drag. . . step, drag. Like he had a limp or polio. But it wasn't quiet. It was loud steps."

All the family members would hear them. They would lie in bed and look up at the ceiling and imagine the ghost walking along. . . step, drag. . . step, drag. . . step, drag. . . .

 But no one ever saw any figure.

"I would hear music," said Katie. "It was like drums and cymbals, like the sounds you would hear from a one-man band. There also was knocking on the doors and you would go to answer and no one would be there."

It was her bedroom that had a back stairway that went up into the attic. One afternoon, Katie and Cassandra were exploring and climbed those stairs. When they arrived at the top of the doorway that led into the attic, they noticed a closet-like room in the center of the building's topmost floor. It was small and painted a bright shade of red.

One door formed the entrance. Katie slowly twisted the knob and shoved the tiny door back.

"It was empty," Katie remembered, "except for a little, child-size, handmade wooden crutch. It was leaning against one corner, only about three feet high. I wanted to take it out and play with it."

But, Barbara added, "I told them, 'No! It belongs to the ghost. That's why he walks like that, why his steps sound so different.' "

Years passed and Luther's presence became an accepted fact of life, a regular part of the Matthews' family routine.

"We would talk to him," Katie said. "It was just like having a friend who was home with you. I would be having breakfast and a plate cabinet would open first, then a food cabinet would open next. And I would say, 'Morning, Luther! Are you hungry? Are you getting your breakfast, Buddy?' "

Referring to a different occasion, when Luther was making noise at night, Cassandra said she would say, "I hear you, Luther!. Now, calm down. It's time to go to bed!"

Barbara added, "I'd say, 'Okay! It's time to stop now,' or 'Ol' Luther's up and about this morning!' If he would open a cupboard, 'Luther must be hungry, he's coming to join us for supper.' Or, if the door would open, 'Luther must have wanted out or needed some fresh air.'"

Arthur's wife, Suzi, was sunbathing on a lounge chair in the back yard, not too far from the farmhouse kitchen door. At her side was Muttley, the family dog, a 55-lb. Golden Retriever. A proud non-believer in Luther and any other ghosts, Suzi told the family to go out on their errands. She had no problem staying home alone that summer afternoon. It was a perfect day to get a suntan.

Soon after the family left, Suzi heard a child's voice, from the house, calling the word: "Mutt-leeee . . . Mutt-leeee," over and over.

The dog went wild, and raced toward the kitchen. It clawed at the wooden door, trying frantically to get into the house.

Suzi put her hands over her ears, closed her eyes, and tried to close out the sound of the piercing, sing-song chant. After several minutes, Suzi couldn't stand it any longer and ran toward the house, opened the back door and let the dog inside.

Immediately, the calling voice of the phantom child stopped.

"She never went into the house," Barbara said, "just grabbed up her stuff, got in her car and drove off. We figure, Luther just wanted to get out of the house and he was fine when Suzi opened the door."

"Now she's a believer," Cassandra said, laughing.

"Some people think you're crazy," admitted Barbara. "It depends on whether you're a believer or not. I always knew there was a presence in the house, but I never felt afraid."

"I didn't take any occasion to be home alone, never liked it," said Katie. "But, when you were home alone and you would hear something, at first, you'd say, 'Oh, God! Someone's got in!' But then you realized it was our ghost, and it was a relief."

Almost a year after she moved away from the farmhouse, Barbara still feels a sense of loss because of the absence of Luther.

"I miss him. Maybe that's why I can't sleep at night," she said. "Maybe I'm looking for Luther, and sometimes I wonder what happened to him."

Katie echoed her mother's feelings. "I miss him, too. It's like, somebody else is going to get him. It makes you feel jealous. They say a lot of times they'll follow you. But I think Luther has something to resolve in the house, and that's why he's still there."

"But you have to understand," Katie added, "there's never been a doubt that we were talking about something real. Luther was real."

"And it wasn't just one of us who heard him," said Cassandra. "It was all of us."

When the family helped Barbara move from the farmhouse in the summer of 1994, Arthur's friend, Tommy, convinced them to pry the nails out of the basement doorway that they had kept sealed up for 20 years.

Slowly, the group descended the worn wooden steps, headed down into the musty, stone walled cellar. They were hoping to get one last glance at the small white coffin that they had sealed up two decades before.

"When they got down there," said Katie, "it was gone."

"Nobody ever questioned how or why." Barbara said, casually. "We figured Luther did what he wanted to with it. You live with them ghosts long enough, you know they do what they want."

Ghosts, Aliens or Soldiers in the Sky?

My good friend George Reynolds of Elk Mills, Md., is, among other things, an expert on UFOs. As director of the Northeast Maryland Chapter of the Mutual UFO Network (MUFON), George is a nationally recognized UFOlogist. He has been interviewed by a number of journalists and authors, as well as television producers working on documentaries about alien abductions, crop circles and UFOs in general. He's been behind the radio microphone, in front of the television camera and at the podium as keynote speaker at conferences around the country.

When George Reynolds speaks about the mysteries surrounding visitors from outer space, experts in the field listen carefully.

With this in mind, I was particularly interested when George called and said he was going to send me a newspaper article entitled "Visions in the Air." I became more attentive when he said it had to do with strange sightings that occurred on Delmarva.

Then he threw in the clincher, "It was written more than 120 years ago."

There was no doubt in my mind that George, also a noted archaeologist and historian, had produced another noteworthy find.

In the mail a few days later, I received a copy of the front page article that appeared in the Oct. 6, 1881, issue of the *The Morning News*, a Wilmington, Del., newspaper. The piece is printed in this chapter in its entirety and unedited, thereby maintaining all its flowery Victorian era verbiage.

While reading the story, I recalled conversations I had had with George. These discussions focused on the fact that some who investigate the paranormal and life in outer space argue that aliens are not a 20th-century mystery. They say the visitors-from-other-planets craze did not begin in 1947, when there were a fair number of reported sightings, including the much publicized (and many believe, covered-up) crash at Roswell, New Mexico.

Some contend that alien sightings have occurred for thousands of years. Some claim that carvings on the walls of caves document these visits, and images of flying discs can be seen in centuries-old paintings.

Certainly, many people tend to explain the cause of strange activities with the offhand statement, and accompanying smile, "Oh, that's just our ghost. Don't worry, it won't bother you. It's friendly."

But, perhaps there's more to these mysterious bumps in the night and sightings of phantoms in the parlor. What if the so-called ghosts or spirits are really aliens from another galaxy far, far away? What if the roaming wraiths are not the restless souls of former residents of the haunted house or victims who lost their souls on a bloody battlefield?

Or maybe, the visions in the night might be a combination of both—alien and phantom—unexplained entities that have joined forces to puzzle and perplex us ignorant Earthlings, as they apparently did in the early fall of 1881.

Read on, and be amazed at what occurred on Delmarva, more than 50 years before Orson Welles terrorized radio listeners with his 1938 broadcast of H.G. Wells' "War of the Worlds."

"Visions in the Air" appears in large bold type at the top left column of the 19th century newspaper.

Just below, in smaller size letters, is the statement: "Soldiers and Angels Seen in the Sky."

And a third, slightly smaller headline adds: "The Strange Appearances as Described by Eye Witnesses in Various Parts of the Peninsula."

One can imagine the reaction of Victorian era readers as they glanced at the northern Delaware newspaper on that fall Thursday morning. For sure, many ignored the competing big stories of the Elkton livestock exhibition at the Cecil County Agricultural Fair and the trio of women from Harrisburg who visited Wilmington. Instead, the father, and master of the home, who certainly was provided with the newspaper before anyone else in the family, probably announced, "Wife, gather the children and listen to this story of strange images in the heavens."

Responding without question, the family sat patiently around the breakfast table, as the patriarch selected passages from the report that he decided were appropriate to share.

> Peninsula people have been seeing ghosts and supernatural objects with alarming frequency during the last three weeks. It is a rather late day to transform the strip of land between the Delaware and Chesapeake Bays into the Isle of Palmos, but circumstances seem to point that way at present. It is of some

consolation to know, however, that if any people are deserving of a look ahead, behind the curtain and into the great unknown, it is the people of Delaware and the Eastern Shore. They have been in this country as long, almost, as anybody else; they can trace their family tree back to the time when the red skins inhabited the region around about Indian River and Baltimore hundreds, and they have at last received their reward.

As usual, it is not the rich man, but the poor man and his children who have seen these supernatural images and ghost-like goblins in the air. The rich man has been busy hoarding pennies for the Michigan sufferers, which he ought to distribute among his farm hands, and the poor man has taken out his revenge in this way.

The first instance of things heavenly having been seen, comes from Royal Oak, Maryland, a small village lying between Pennsylvania on the north, and the Atlantic Ocean on the south, and equally situated between the Chesapeake and Delaware bays, with, perhaps a slight preponderance of proximity in favor of the former.

A little girl, some three weeks ago, living in the village, saw after night-fall, before the moon was fairly up above the horizon, whole platoons of angels slowly marching and counter-marching to and fro in the clouds, their white robes and helmets glistening with a weird light. At intervals the heavenly visitors would dance mournfully, as if to the sound of unseen music, and certainly unheard music. She rushed in to her parents and declared that the heavens had been spread and betrayed to her visions sights somewhat premature, as regards time, and then sank down in affright.

Her father, to satisfy his doubting mind, went out and was rewarded with a sight of the unearthly spectacle. The news of the mystery quickly spread from mouth to mouth, house to house, and in an incredibly short space of time the inhabitants were out en masse gazing in open-mouthed astonishment, while the white robed hosts, seemingly offended at the immense amount of genuine astonishment and wonder they were unearthing, slowly faded from sight, leaving Royal Oak a firm believer, from the little girl who was first on the spot, to the squire in his little office behind the church, in ghosts and winged goblins. But the phenomena seem to have been especially manifest in Sussex County, Delaware.

Monday night, two weeks ago, William West, a farmer, living near Georgetown, the county seat, saw at a time almost identical with the appearance of the vision at Royal Oak, bands of soldiers of great size, equipped with dazzling uniforms, their musket steels quivering and shimmering in the pale weird light that seemed to be everywhere, marching with military precision up and down unseen avenues and presenting arms at the sound of unheard commands.

The vision was of startling distinctness and lasted long enough to be seen by a number of West's neighbors, who, after the unearthly military had taken its departure and been swallowed up in thin air, retailed the strange story to their eager friends, who had not been so fortunate as they. An account of the occurrence appeared the next week in the *Georgetown Inquirer*. But strangest of all, a man named Coverdale, who was driving through the country along a lonely road, at the same time, being then several miles away from West's house, and in an entirely different direction, saw to his astonishment and alarm, the same band of soldiers in their faultless uniforms, so accurately described by the *Inquirer*. Many people living near Laurel, many miles away, situated in the lower end of the Peninsula, saw the same extraordinary phenomena at the same time.

There are not a few who refuse to regard it as an optical illusion, but strongly cling to the opinion that they have seen the martial band of soldiers, the departed comrades of the martyred president, coming down from Heaven to welcome home their well beloved chieftain. A few even go so far as to say, in spite of the ridicule of their associates, that they distinctly saw in the midst of the soldiers, and conspicuous by reason of the size and commanding presence, the hero president himself pale, but with every feature distinctly and vividly portrayed. This, of course, is the way the paper related the affair, but there is no doubt of the fact that there were many who thought they saw Garfield in the clouds.*

In Talbot county the illusion was seen by numbers. A farmer living near Clara's Point, on going out into his yard after dark saw, as he related it afterwards to his neighbors, angels and soldiers marching side by side in the clouds, wheeling, and going through every evolution with military precision and absolutely life-like and natural. He was so deceived and impressed by the unnatural appearance that he rushed into the house and brought out his wife, who, in turn, saw the spectacle, and became as firmly convinced of its reality as her husband had been.

In this city, a little girl saw angels marching to and fro among the clouds at about the same time, and breathlessly carried the startling news to her parents, who were in the house at the time and who refused to believe such a thing possible until they went out and saw the spectacle for themselves. Also, in a number of other places throughout the State and Peninsula, these strange and supernatural appearances were seen by many people, among them the superstitious, who have industriously circulated the belief among the credulous that the world will speedily come to an end; while there were others who saw in those creatures in the air, portents of pestilence and famine, war and bloodshed.

Viewed in any light the simultaneous appearance over so large an extent of country as that comprising the Peninsula, of these mirages of the air is to say the least, very singular. So far as known there have been no bodies of soldiery under discipline within a radius of a hundred miles, and yet the shadowy soldiers seen in the clouds must have had their counterparts in living and moving men, but where no one knows.

The more the matter is inquired into, the more unfathomable it gets. It has been offered in explanation that the solders seen were but the reflection of the lonely and weary brigade now toiling its way to Yorktown; but this is insufficient, since the company in question, although it recently marched through lower Pennsylvania, is now too far away to cast such a long shadow.**

Again, it is said that the vision is prophetic, and that it represents Delaware's militia, brigadier-generals, colonels and all as they will appear when they reach Yorktown and fairly begin to amaze the honest natives from the other States. This explanation however, is faulty, in that no account is given of the angels, who appeared with the soldiery in a number of instances, the tide of angels being mixed up with the Blue Hen's chickens being a decidedly unnatural one. There has thus far, however, been no satisfactory solution given to the series of mysterious specters in the sky.

*References to the departed President James A. Garfield, who was shot on July 2, 1881, in Washington, D.C., and died Sept. 19 of that year.

**References to Yorktown most probably allude to a centennial march commemorating the Revolutionary War Battle of Yorktown, which took place Oct. 6-19, 1781.

The Room

Northern New Jersey, west of New York City. That's where I was told this story occurred—in the country, fairly far from the hustle and bustle of modern, 21st-century workday life. The now-deserted, but dramatically improved, property still stands amidst farms and forests, rural fence posts and rusty stop signs along less traveled roads. It's a calm area that is fortunate to exist beyond the crawling, ever-extending reach of suburban development.

The entire episode is the result of what appeared to be a dream come true.

No doubt, similar inspirational scenarios are played out every spring weekend, when enthusiastic couples eagerly head for the country to escape the congested city. The warm breezes that follow winter lure Saturday refugees toward nature's freshly awakened treasures like a swarm of flies landing on fresh-cut watermelon, like a column of ants charging a cake crumb, like a pack of dogs bounding for juicy, unattended slices of sirloin.

In this case, our young couple, both in their early thirties, found an unnoticed gem of a piece of property. They decided to restore the deserted structure to its former, vibrant, colorful existence.

But, as we will see, sometimes the past isn't worth salvaging.

This is particularly true if the property was the stage for an action so horrible that the essence of evil and phantoms of pain remained buried, and, for so very long, forgotten.

In this case, it would have been better had the structure been left in a state of neglect, leaving the cause of the trouble at sleep.

❖   ❖   ❖

Cheryl (not her real name) said she has a friend who moved into a deserted farmhouse located somewhere in north Jersey, in what remains of the forests and woodlands between New Providence and the Delaware River.

I asked Cheryl to be more specific, but she declined, adding, "I promised I wouldn't let anyone know where the house is located. After all, my friend wants to sell it and hasn't been successful yet. And as I've heard you often say, 'If it's a private residence, don't let anyone know that it's haunted.' "

I nodded, indicating that I understood her friend's concern. I also assured Cheryl that no reader of her story was going to be able to find out which old restored farmhouse was the site of the ghostly activity.

"Good," she said, obviously satisfied, and immediately began to get into the meat and potatoes of her spooky tale.

I'd known Cheryl for about 10 years. She used to work as a reporter. We had met on a few of my cemetery tours. She's charming, well spoken and, unlike a lot of my sources, a paranormal nonbeliever. She admitted she likes to read and hear about the unexplained, but hasn't been convinced that there's anything more to it than coincidences and people's wild imaginations.

Cheryl's skepticism is why her story intrigued me. She's one of the last persons that I thought would be a source of a ghostly tale.

She said her friend Kathy and her husband, Paul, bought a farmette of about 20 acres. They wanted to grow some Christmas trees, have some privacy and get out of the modern suburban townhouse where they had lived for a number of years. They knew they would have to commute farther to work, but decided it was worth the daily hassle to live in a setting they loved.

She said the couple found the location and land they wanted, but the house was ready to fall over.

"It was a wreck," Cheryl said. "I told them they were crazy to buy the place. And if they did, I told them to knock the building down and start all over again. But they didn't listen to me. They spent a fortune fixing the old place up."

I replied that doing so wasn't that unusual. Lots of city folks head into the county and take on the role of gentlemen farmers. Plus, if they had the money to burn, why not use it to save an old building? It's almost a public service.

"Well, they saved more than the building," Cheryl said, waving her hands in the air. "My friend, Kathy, thinks they rejuvenated a few of the former residents."

It took more than a year to get the house into a livable condition. The couple moved in while the construction crew was working on the house. For more than two months, Kathy spent her days at the home while craftsmen tried to complete the finishing work on the restored home.

"Everything was going fairly well, other than the routine delays," Cheryl said, "until the tools started going missing."

Cheryl explained that hammers, rules, packs of nails and even power saws and power drills would disappear.

"A worker would place an item down," Cheryl said, "and within a few seconds the tool would be gone. In the beginning, they thought one of the guys was playing a joke on the others. But as the frequency increased the level of frustration and arguing got worse. One day, my friend had to separate two guys in her front yard who were ready to go at it with two-by-fours, claiming each had stolen the other's hammer. She told me it was downright scary."

I asked if they ever found the tools.

"That's the strange thing," Cheryl said. "The very next day, or two at the most, the missing tools would be on the floor in the middle of the second floor room that overlooked the front entrance of the house. That room has a great view. From the massive window, you can look down the long tree-lined lane and see anyone coming up to the front of the house. There's a rocking chair facing the window. If I had that house, I would sit there all day and read and enjoy my mini-estate."

Apparently, that's what Kathy had planned to do. She turned the room into her study. It was bright and filled with bookshelves and plants that were placed there to benefit from morning sunlight.

But it also was the room where the tools turned up. And other things, strange things, happened there.

"They weren't major incidents," Cheryl said, "just little, odd, quirky things that took place from time to time. Like the room was often very cold. I noticed it the first time I was in the home. It was the only spot in the main portion of the farmhouse that was 15 or 20 degrees colder than the rest of the building. Kathy also told me that the door would never seem to stay shut, even when she was sure it had been locked. But the strangest thing was the sound of soft, little footsteps in the room."

Footsteps?

"Yes," Cheryl replied. "But not heavy ones, like a normal grown person. Very soft, almost a patter and quick, like a little person—like a baby or young child. But," she paused a moment, "Kathy heard them when she was in the room, not when she was downstairs. She told me that she would sit at her desk, hear them running across the hardwood floor and turn around, very quickly.

Of course, there was no one there, but she got to the point of looking on the floor, to see if she could see any damp small footprints on the polished wood."

I asked Cheryl if her friend, the house owner, ever told anyone else about what she had heard.

Cheryl laughed before she answered. "She told her husband and he said she was 'nuts.' But, then men often say that to their wives. It's to be expected. Of course, Paul didn't believe any of this. Kathy told me he was either in denial or deaf. That is, until the day he heard a sound in the room, opened the door and saw the rocker, that usually sits facing the front, second-floor window, moving back and forth. Of course it was empty but was moving in a steady rhythm, and no one was in there and no wind was making it happen. That got his attention."

I told Cheryl that he probably said it was the wind, to convince himself he wasn't "nuts."

She was stunned for a moment, ready to ask how I knew that was exactly what had happened. Then she caught herself and realized I had heard tales of unbelieving husbands many times before.

"Eventually," Cheryl said, "Kathy stopped going into the room, other than to water her plants. It wasn't 'user friendly,' she told me. Storage boxes began to claim the open spaces. She kept the door locked as best she could. No one was enjoying the view from the large window. At least that's what she thought."

One afternoon, late in the day, Cheryl said Kathy was standing in the front field, talking to a landscaper. The local man had been called in to offer a bid on a project. Kathy's back was to the house. While conversing, the visitor paused, and waved up at the house. His eyes were focused on the second-floor window, the one in the cold room with the footsteps.

Kathy asked him what he was doing, and the man responded that he was waving back at the older lady who had been looking down from the window. He assumed it was Kathy's mother.

"Kathy told me she turned her head so fast she thought it would snap," Cheryl said. "Of course, Kathy didn't see anyone, and she was in no mood to re-enter the house alone. So she asked the man to come in with her. She led him up to the room on the second floor. She unlocked the door, went inside and there was no one present. Except, the empty rocker was moving back and forth."

The contractor didn't stay long when Kathy told him the whole story.

He also never came back to follow up about the job. That afternoon, Kathy locked up the place and waited for Paul in her car at the bottom of their lane. She told him she wouldn't go back in that house alone.

The landscaper described the woman he had seen in the window as "old and wearing a black dress and hood." He added that he thought she might have had something in her arms, perhaps a blanket or maybe even a baby. But of that he couldn't be sure.

Kathy convinced Paul that they should spend a few days with a relative. Reluctantly, he agreed. When they went back to the house, Kathy said, it was never the same. There was a "bothersome presence" in their home.

Paul received more daytime calls to his work number from his uneasy wife, who began to avoid climbing the stairs to the second floor. Eventually, if no one else was home, she refused to go upstairs and began calling her friend, Cheryl, inviting her to come over for more frequent visits.

Paul was beginning to become annoyed, and the couple began fighting several times a week. Their dream castle had turned into a genuine haunted house.

"I began avoiding my own phone," Cheryl said. "Kathy's problem was becoming mine, especially when Paul stopped answering her calls to his office. And I, too, began going crazy. I actually got caller ID on every phone in the house. And, I hate to say this, but I would not answer if I saw Kathy was on the other end. It made me feel guilty, but I had to keep my sanity. If I went over there every time she called, I'd be living there."

Cheryl's guilt level went off the chart when she drove by her friend's mini-estate one day and spotted a "for sale" sign on the front lawn, near the split rail fence beside the gate.

"At first I couldn't believe it," Cheryl said, "I wanted to drive up the lane and apologize and find out what was going on. I really believed it was my fault."

When she learned the unsettling events that caused the couple's decision to dispose of the property, Cheryl realized there was nothing she could have done to stop the eerie circumstances that led up to the final, shocking haunting.

One evening, a steady, rocking sound awakened Kathy about 2 o'clock in the morning. It was coming from the haunted, cold room down the hall. She tried to awaken Paul, but he didn't respond to her nudges and pleadings.

A few minutes later he jumped from his bed when he heard her piercing scream.

"Kathy told me she stumbled into the hall," Cheryl said. "She rubbed her eyes and patted the hallway walls, looking for the light switch. But when she found the control, it didn't work. She flicked it several times, but it would not turn on."

Persistent, Kathy continued down the hallway, heading toward the rocking chair sound, placed the key in the lock and shoved open the door. Again, she hit the wall switch to illuminate the room, but it also didn't work.

"She told me that, for some unexplained reason, she suddenly didn't care about the broken lights," Cheryl said. "There was a full moon, spreading a glow through the massive window. It was beaming in on the rocking chair that was moving back and forth. But, this time it wasn't empty. Kathy said she was pulled toward the far end of the room as if there was a magical, tempting lure.

"She said there was a figure, wearing a dark cloak and hood, facing out toward the window. Whoever was there, in that cold room had its back to Kathy, who approached slowly. When she got next to the figure, she noticed there was something in the cloaked figure's arms. Whether it was a baby, or a small child. Kathy wasn't sure."

Apparently, the sight of the child pulled Kathy out of her trance. As she began to try to move backwards, to return toward the doorway, the figure in the chair grabbed onto the younger woman's wrist.

"Kathy described the hand as 'ice cold, like a death grip,' " Cheryl recalled. "She told me she tried to scream, to pull away, but nothing would function. Her voice wouldn't work. Her legs and arms were heavy, like lead, like when you're having a nightmare. She couldn't even move in slow motion. Then, while she was stuck in place, the black cloaked figure turned toward her and pulled back the cloth that was covering the creature in its arms."

That's when she screamed. And, at that moment when her voice reached her husband's ears, all the lights in the house came on and the figures in the rocking chair disappeared.

"I got chills when Kathy told me what happened that night," Cheryl said. "Besides the lights and cold and rocking chair, the worst part, what she remembers most of all, are the faces of the old woman and the child.

"She said the woman looked like the wicked witch in Walt Disney's *Snow White*. But the creature in her arms was 'horrifying,' because it was a baby's body with an old person's face. And the face was evil, twisted and wrinkled, like a deformed little person, what you might expect of an old troll or elf. It didn't seem human. And, one half of its face, the entire right side, was burnt like it had been charred in a fire."

Terrified, Cheryl wanted to leave the house that night. But, her husband refused and told her she was over reacting. That it was just a "bad dream."

He offered to go into the room and prove there was nothing to be afraid of.

Kathy waited in her bedroom less than 15 minutes when her husband returned and told her to begin packing.

"He refused to tell her anything until they were out of the house," Cheryl said. "Later that night, when they were settled in a motel room, he told her he had intended to see if there was anything to his wife's story, so he sat in the rocker. After only a minute, he noticed something move outside the large window.

"When he stood up and walked to the glass, he peered out, with his face up against the window pane, trying to see out into the darkness. Suddenly, the old woman appeared, but she was floating, outside the house, tapping with this claw-like finger on the second-floor window, as if she wanted him to let her in."

Cheryl said apparently that was proof enough, and Kathy's husband rushed her into the car and drove out of their haunted estate.

Kathy and Paul have asked themselves a dozen times if their renovations could have been the cause of the mysterious events. They read somewhere that construction activity can agitate ghosts or encourage hauntings. They also thought the spirits might have been attracted by the antique rocker they had found in the basement and restored, or more accurately "awakened."

Cheryl paused, then added, "I heard on one of those cable shows, about the paranormal, that certain things never die, never cease to exist in some form. These spirit experts claimed that unusual, unexplained entities have a special ability to come back, many years after they were thought to have left their earthly surroundings. They said these ghosts can manifest themselves to the living, especially those who have followed after them and who live in the home where the ghosts lived when they were alive."

I agreed and added that people will probably never know if these unusual sightings or manifestations are the energy charged remnants of tragic events or simply strong willed beings who have some extra sense of affection or attraction with their past.

"But," I added, "whether we know them by name or not, it seems obvious they want to make their presence known."

❖ ❖ ❖

After that disturbing evening, Cheryl said the terrified couple returned to their home only once, to direct a team of movers that packed up their belongings.

Kathy and Paul gave the rocker to one of the fellows working on the moving crew. He noticed that the antique was remaining behind. When he realized the owners weren't taking it, the man asked if he could have it.

Rather than explain the entire story, the weary couple said they were exhausted with the whole horrible dream home experience and agreed to pass along the possessed possession to a new, unsuspecting host. Later, they felt guilty and decided that their spur-of-the-moment decision hadn't been a good idea. But, realizing it would have been very difficult to track down the new owner of the haunted rocker, they let nature take its course.

"It's out there somewhere," Cheryl said. "Now it's somebody else's problem. But, who can say for sure if it was the house or rocker that was the cause of the strange events. Maybe it was something that happened on that site, on the land. Who will ever know for sure?"

True.

Who will ever be able to discover the identity of the old woman, the name of the deformed, troll-like child or even the eventual location of the "free" antique troubled rocker?

Maybe no one should ever know the whole truth.

Surely, some mysteries are best left unanswered.

Tombstones Tales

Much can be learned about
the dead, and those who
loved them, by reading the
interesting inscriptions carved in smooth slabs of stone.

For centuries, these manmade monuments have served as a
tribute to departed loved ones and also marked the final resting
sites of those who have left this hectic world behind.

Warning Carved in Stone Chestertown, Md.

An inscription on a sample tombstone marker offers passing
drivers sensible advice. At Kirby Memorials—which has been
doing business at the intersection of Maple Avenue and Cross
Street in Chestertown since 1892—the small white tombstone
reads:

"Drive With Care, We Can Wait."

Can't Argue With This Welsh Tract Church, Newark, Del.

Many years ago, companies that sold and carved cemetery
memorials and monuments offered their customers the opportunity
to select from a number of books with verses and popular sayings to
adorn the face of family tombstones.

One popular verse read:

"Remember me as you pass by,
As you are now so once was I.
As I am now so you must be,
Prepare yourself to follow me."

Hobbyists and artists who visit historic and older cemeteries
seeking interesting epitaphs for their tombstones rubbings have
noted this same inscription in various graveyards throughout the
Delmarva Peninsula and mid-Atlantic region.

According to the late Jeanette Rust McDonnal, a long time resident of Methodist Manor in Milford, Del., this specific eternal warning can be found on a leaning tombstone in the churchyard of the Welsh Tract Church, located south of Newark, Del., just off Route 896.

The greenish-gray, slate gravestone still stands to the east of the rear portion of the old brick church.

Its inscription states:

"In Memory of Richard Thomas, who departed this life
Nov. the 20, 1753.
Aged 71 years.
"Remember man as thou stands by,
As thou art now so once was I.
As I am now so thou must be,
Therefore prepare to follow me."

Mrs. McDonnal, a member of the University of Delaware Class of 1931 recalled an incident that occurred while she was attending the Women's College in Newark.

Several young ladies were walking through the graveyard when the epitaph noted above caught the eye of one clever student. The young lady stopped and, with a piece of chalk, added a few witty lines on the ample space at the bottom of the stone.

Her poetic addition read:

"To follow you
I'm not content,
Until I know,
Which way you went."

While the student's classmates were quiet impressed, Mrs. McDonnal recalled that an administrator at the college discovered what had occurred and she had a less enthusiastic response.

The young lady poet was sent back to the site of her crime and, it is said, was instructed to clean the stone and erase her creative verse—by using a toothbrush and water.

That incident, however, remains a pleasant memory that will live longer than some of the messages etched in stone that are waging a losing battle against weather and the elements.

From a Graveyard Guide
St. Peter's Church
Lewes, Del.

There are a number of interesting tombstones in the grave-yard surrounding Saint Peter's Church, located in the center of the shopping district in Lewes, Delaware. The current church, built in 1851, is the third to be constructed since the congregation was established in 1681.

To assist curious visitors, A *Supplementary Guide to the Churchyard* is available in the rear of the sanctuary. This one-page flier includes a site diagram and detailed information on 18 marked gravestones. Perhaps two of the most unusual are:

The Pilot's Anchor

The grave marked as #11 in the guide designates the grave of Capt. Henry F. McCracken, a Delaware River and Bay pilot. In 1868, his descendants responded to his request that his anchor be buried with him. A small metal tip, said to be a section of the fluke—the pointed part of the anchor that is designed to grab the sea bottom—can be seen protruding from the earth at the foot of the captain's grave.

30 Days has February?

The grave designated #4 in Saint Peter's flier, known as the "February 30th Stone." needs no explanation. The inscription proclaims:

> **"In memory of Elizabeth H. Cullen,
> born February 30th, A.D. 1760
> and departed this life
> September 30th, A.D. 1830 . . . . "**

Stately Affection

Odd Fellows Cemetery
Camden, Del.

An interesting tombstone off Route 10 outside Camden, Delaware marks the final resting place of Raymond Walter Dill, born on August 13, 1920, and died on August 3, 1985.

Mr. Dill's tombstone stands at the end of a curving roadway, toward the south end of the cemetery. Although it is not the tallest granite marker, nor the most expensive eternal monument, it is, many believe, among the most distinctive to be found on Delmarva.

Raymond Dill's unique tombstone is carved into the shape of the state of Delaware, and its markings designate the boundary lines of New Castle, Kent and Sussex counties.

According to the deceased's brother, Martin Dill of Felton, Mr. Raymond Dill was a long-time Dover area resident who had an extensive collection of items related to Delaware history. It included more than 13,000 postcards of the First State as well as several hundred books.

"He loved and knew the state of Delaware," Martin Dill said of his brother, who had been involved in conducting research on all of the cemeteries in Kent County. After his death, Martin Dill and his wife, Elizabeth Bostick Dill, completed the project and published the book *Souls in Heaven, Names in Stone.* They sought out 379 reported cemeteries in Kent County and recorded 229 of them. The others, many small farm resting plots, were destroyed or lost when they were covered over by residential developers and those with agribusiness interests.

More than 1,400 pages of records are included in the book's two volumes, used for historical and genealogical research.

For more information on *Souls in Heaven, Names in Stone,* write to Martin Dill at Route 1, Box 12, Felton, DE 19943.

Short Sightings

Here are a few unusual incidents and legends that are worth sharing but which are not long enough to be presented as separate chapters.

Tangier Terror

Tangier Island, Virginia

My friend Sarah told me a story about events that occurred at the home of her brother, Harold, and her sister-in-law, Betty, (not their real names), who live on Tangier Island, an isolated portion of Virginia in the Chesapeake Bay. Since the couple claims its home is built on an Indian burial ground, unusual activity at their residence occurs a bit more frequently than at other sites on the island and on the mainland.

The first ghost they saw "wasn't a good ghost," Sarah said. "And believe me, they have seen plenty. All the other ghosts were good and just like to tease you, they told me. But the first one was the worst."

Sarah said Harold and Betty had fallen asleep one evening while watching television. He was snoozing in a lounge chair and she was sleeping on a sofa located on the other side of the room.

"When Harold woke up," Sarah said, "he had left his chair and was standing over his wife choking her, and she was making gurgling sounds. He couldn't believe he was doing this. Betty pointed to his chest, and when he looked down he saw a large black-and-white snake, about six-feet long, wrapped around him. He took his hands off of Betty and got hold of the snake, and Betty ran into the other room and got out *The Bible*."

By the time Betty returned to the living room and started to read passages from *The*

Bible, the snake began to leave her husband's body. As it slithered across the floor and headed into the kitchen, Betty continued to read holy verses aloud and the couple followed behind the serpent.

"They followed the snake from the living room to the kitchen," Sarah said. "When the snake got to the back door, it disappeared like a puff of smoke. That was more than three years ago. They have been afraid to tell anyone, and the two of them didn't speak a word about it until they visited me at my place. And they haven't seen the snake again since that night, but they have a copy of *The Bible* in every room, in case it were to happen again."

Cleaning House
Kent County, Delaware

After conducting a cemetery tour in Kent County, Delaware, two ladies—Peggy and Joyce—shared their unusual experience, while cleaning an old mansion outside of a nearby town.

The women, who work cleaning residences and businesses, said they were hired to straighten up a large deserted home located on the outskirts of a sleepy rural town. They were told the building was going to be sold and that it needed a "once over."

After cleaning one of the main first-floor parlors, they moved to an adjacent room. However, about a half hour later, when they passed through the room they had cleaned earlier, they noticed that a number of items were out of place.

"Cushions were tossed on the floor, a lamp was knocked over and a chair was sitting on its side," Peggy said. "I knew there was something wrong, because everything was fine when we completed the room before, and no one had been in the house. We hadn't heard a thing. No one came into the house while we were there."

Looking over at her friend, Peggy added, "So I straightened out what was knocked over, but then Joyce wanted to leave."

"No kidding!" Joyce replied. "No way I was going to do anything else in that place. I was on my way out the door. Whether it was a ghost or burglar, there wasn't enough money for me to do any more work there. Plus," she added, "we still had to go and do the top floor. You weren't going to get me trapped up there."

Peggy, who stressed that she eventually had to leave because her partner refused to continue, said, "I wasn't going to stay in there alone. I would have finished the job if Miss Sissy Face here had stayed. I told her she didn't even have to clean, just keep an eye out while I did all the work, but she wouldn't hear a word from me. She was out the front door just like that!"

Defending her decision, Joyce added, "When we went back to the real estate office, the woman wasn't surprised. In fact, she told us that we weren't the first cleaners who ran out of that house."

Apparently, the real estate agent responsible for the home's sale said a previous cleaner she had hired had reported hearing a piano playing in the house. But, there was no piano in the home, hadn't been for about 50 years.

"But," Joyce said, smiling, as if her fears were confirmed, "the woman at the real estate office said the owner, who died in the house many years ago, used to play the piano all the time. So I guess ghost piano players can play ghost pianos."

Pieces of String
Downstate Delaware

Several years ago I visited an elderly fellow in downstate Delaware. During our phone conversation to set up the visit, I learned that his experiences were quite unusual and I asked a University of Delaware student, named Kenny, to accompany me to the interview.

We arrived at the man's home, located at the edge of a small country town, about 7 p.m. It was late spring and there was still about an hour left of daylight. Lex (not his real name) was in is seventies and a widower. He lived alone and welcomed us into his home. Beyond the edge of his driveway and small yard was a very large stretch of flat fields. A few distant farmhouses and barns accented the level landscape.

Lex waved his hand and directed us into his kitchen, led us down a narrow hall and pointed to a few empty chairs in the parlor. Kenny and I took seats side by side and began to listen to our host's tales.

A retiree, Lex said he had plenty of time to read and work on his various hobbies, which included woodcarving and stamp collecting. He also spent several hours at the local barbershop meeting place a few days a week "keeping up on things." We allowed him to talk a while before I began to steer the conversation in a more spirited direction.

"What about your ghosts?" I eventually asked.

It didn't take much prompting to get Lex to spin out his spirited stories. Enthusiastically, he switched subjects and began talking about the group of ghosts that visited him nightly.

"They dance in the kitchen," he said, pointing toward the adjoining room. "But after a few nights," he continued, "they begin to come out here, in the parlor. I hate when they take my TV *Guide* and move it all around so I can't find it."

At this point in the conversation, Kenny began looking in my direction, wondering what to think. This was his first such interview session. It was obvious that the focus of the conversation was quite different from Kenny's experiences while writing articles about his professors' books for the college newspaper.

During Lex's story about his night visitors, he said the newer ghosts tend to stay back until they got to know the lay of the land. However, there were so many in the kitchen on some evenings that the house owner could hardly see the other end of the room.

I asked when they usually appeared, and Lex replied that activity reached its peak about 2 o'clock in the morning. He immediately invited both of us to stay overnight and see for ourselves.

My student companion and I had not planned a ghostly overnight and declined, but we told Lex we would consider a return visit.

He described his phantom roommates as mostly young and attired in old-fashioned clothing. The men wore odd looking caps and vests and the women were small, with thin waists, long hair and "were darn good looking young things."

I got the impression Lex was a ladies' man.

"You have to sit very still,' Lex advised us, explaining that he learned that any abrupt movement tended to run them off. Therefore, when the ghost gang first appeared, he was careful to remain stiff as a statue.

"That's only until they get comfortable with things," he said. "After a while, you can even get up and move around. But in the beginning, you can't move a muscle."

Kenny's eyes widened as Lex rattled off his experiences, about how the ghosts danced, partied and later moved around small objects and rearranged furniture. Since we were new to his scene, Lex offered a suggestion that would allow us to communicate during the night without speaking and avoid scaring off his spooky guests.

"We will all sit here, in seats beside each other," Lex said. "We can tie pieces of string to each other's fingers. Then, whichever one of us sees the first ghost, he can move a finger just a little bit and tug on the string. That will alert the other two, and we can look up and watch. That way, we won't spook them off when they show up."

I told Lex that was a very clever idea, and one I had not heard before.

Kenny's eyes had grown to their physical limit. Since the clock had chimed 9 p.m., I decided it was time to wrap up the interview and head north.

Lex kindly offered to let us stay on watch with him until the ghosts' usual early morning arrival. In fact, he said if I had to go he would let Kenny stay the night and give him a ride north in the morning.

Kenny broke his silence and declined the offer, explaining he had "an early morning class and tests to study for."

I said if it hadn't been for Kenny, I would have agreed to stay, but I was responsible for the lad's return.

Lex invited us to stop by any time. No notice necessary.

I had planned to return and check out Lex's claims. But, as the years passed, other priorities consumed my time and I never arranged a follow-up. Occasionally, I've driven by Lex's home and have been tempted to stop and knock on his kitchen door. I don't know if he still lives there or not, if he would remember me or if he continues to host his assemblage of night visitors.

Part of me wants to go back and sit with Lex, to prove or disprove his claim. But something else tells me to leave the elderly ghost host alone and allow him and his visitors their privacy.

Red Signal Near the Water

Conowingo, Maryland

According to legend, the ghosts of a band of murdered slaves haunt the riverbank of the Susquehanna River, north of the Conowingo Dam, in Cecil County, Maryland.

The Mason-Dixon Line, which runs east and west, is a short walk north of present day U.S. Route 1 in that northern section of the county. It was the unofficial designation marking the separation of the Northern and Southern States during the Civil War. Even today, people recognize that centuries-old boundary, drawn in the late 1700s by surveyors Charles Mason and Jeremiah Dixon.

During the War Between the States—or War of Northern Aggression, as it is still labeled by residents of the Confederacy—slaves traveling along the Underground Railroad followed the

North Star, heading for freedom. One of their first objectives was to reach the state of Pennsylvania.

Secret trails throughout the Delmarva Peninsula were the escape routes. Many of these hidden paths led to Wilmington, Delaware, and Philadelphia, two major cites where abolitionists were numerous and safe haven was waiting for any slave that made it that far.

Other runaways moved through the marshes and guts along the western side of the peninsula, following the wooded, winding banks of the Susquehanna River.

No one knows how many fugitives arrived in the promised land of Pennsylvania. Nor is there an accurate number of those who perished at the hands of slavenappers and Southern sympathizers. One can only imagine how many terrified escapees died from exposure to the elements--some freezing to death during harsh winters, others succumbing to illness and disease in humid summers. Their remains rest unmarked, unnoticed and long forgotten, somewhere in the ground along the northern border of Maryland's Eastern Shore.

One story, however, persists. It tells of a band of slaves, heading north along the mighty Susquehanna. They were sailing on a makeshift raft, probably traveling at night, when darkness helped to mask their flight. They were working against time, trying to avoid notice by spies and capture by bounty hunters. The frightened fugitives worked together, heading toward the top of the Chesapeake Bay and straining against the waters that were rushing south through the rocky rapids at Smith's Falls.

A red light was their objective. Friendly abolitionists used the colored lantern to mark a safe landing site. If the slaves made it to shore at that point, they would be given shelter, food and, most of all, be led to a safe station house. After a brief rest, they could regroup and head further north.

Their primary goal was to travel out of the long reach of their masters and others interested in claiming them as a prize to be bound, gagged and delivered like property to be traded in for hard cash.

Unfortunately, on this night all did not go as planned.

The red light burned. The signal was seen. The raft made it to shore.

But the faces beside the glowing lamp were not friendly.

Slave hunters had gotten word of the plan, taken the abolitionists' place and waited patiently for the escapees to appear.

No one knows what occurred when the frightened blacks met the unfriendly whites. Some say the slaves resisted and were killed and buried in an unmarked mass grave.

Others believe the greedy bounty hunters didn't kill their prey, worth more alive than dead. Instead, the hunters bound their captives and sold them back into slavery earning a healthy profit.

Either way, the road to freedom ended at the red light.

Some locals claim the moans of the raft of doomed slaves can be heard at night, floating across the black surface of the Susquehanna River, especially when a solitary, red ghost light appears in the woods, just above the shoreline.

Elmer Tyson
Eastern Shore Gravedigger

Elmer Tyson, was a big burly bear of a man. Each day he would climb out of the rectangular hole he had spent the day carving into the clay and sand-coated earth. It was regulation size: 8 foot long, 3 foot 2 inches wide and 4-1/2 feet deep.

His wife, Emma, she would often put her hands around the shovel that Elmer was grabbing for support. She pushed down on the smooth handle and pressed the metal tip into the ground, so he could grab it for support as he climbed out of the hole.

The couple, both in their early 60s, lived out on the lower Eastern Shore, out in Dorchester County, for a while. They spent some time near a few relatives in Sussex County, Del., too.

They had been married for 42 years. Passed a lot of their working time together, almost each day for 20 years in graveyards. You see, Elmer was a gravedigger.

He started in the business when he was 16, while he was still in high school, helping his father and grandfather with their work. That was in the late 1940s.

He was young then, not quite as big as he got to be later. But surely almost every bit as strong.

It was natural that he carried on the family business, tending to plots for outlying mission churches and small crossroads and towns. They were accounts that the Tysons had started diggin' on at the turn of the century.

Take a drive on the back roads of Downstate Delaware and the Quiet Counties on the Eastern Shore—away from Routes 301 or 13 or 113— and you'll pass scores of small, secluded church-yards, surrounded by cemeteries. Many of which are still in use.

When you see them, you'll know you're in Tyson territory.

They's little villages and hamlets with working class names—in and around places called Pepperbox, Spence, Trappe, Hardscrabble, Golts, Wango, Chance and Zion.

Whether the cattails were standing tall or the geese were flocking in to get away from the cold weather, it didn't matter. These places all needed tending, all throughout the year. And Elmer and the Tyson family did a lot of that work.

In the real old days—when he would do it all by hand—a pick, shovel and lantern were all he needed. Oh, and a pry bar, in case he had to shove it under the headstone and move the granite marker back, to make a little more room to dig the hole.

In those earlier days, before the Tysons came along, there was usually a hunched over fella from the village who rang the bell for services on Sundays and tended to funerals during the week. He would look after the churchyard, do some basic cleaning and landscaping and dig the graves when they needed to be dug.

But things began to change about 1960, and by the last two decades of the 20th century most of the old timers were gone, wandered off or were dead themselves. Nobody was left behind to do that final job that had to be done.

So Elmer and Emma took over, did a lot of the maintenance chores, too.

Large, big-city and suburban cemeteries had their own staff peo-ple. But the small town churches and country, out-of-the-way chapels still needed to be tended—mowed, weeded and, at times, dug.

That's how Elmer and Emma spend their time. Sometimes seven days a week.

105

"You can't tell nobody not to die on a certain day," Elmer often would say. "So, sometimes, you got to get out there on a weekend and do the diggin' for a Monday buryin'. Ain't no way around it. No way at all."

In the winter, though, when the ground was frozen and the bodies were backed up waiting for burials, and the undertakers and families was a callin' and pressuring for him to get the holes dug, Elmer was known to use a jackhammer to break through the three-foot layer of frozen soil. He had to use it to get below the frost line, but that only happened a few years, that he was able to recall.

"Some of them small places, they would call me to open a grave about five times a year," he said. "That's 'cause the dying business was slow out in the country, less people in the congregations. Fewer and fewer every year it seemed. But the weeds still grew in the summer and the leaves still came down in the fall. So, the way I figured, it always seemed to even out pretty fair."

Elmer's arms were wide, thick as the trunks of small trees. His voice was quiet, reflecting the peace of the small cemeteries and secluded hillsides where he spent most of his waking hours. His face, weathered from decades of time spent with the elements, had the look of a tombstone, soft and worn in some spots, ragged and rough in others.

As years passed, a lot of the work started to be done with machinery. Elmer said a backhoe allowed him to do up to five, sometimes even seven, graves a day. But many places—historic churchyards with stone or brick walls around them, or them with narrow gates, where the machines couldn't enter—called for the old-fashioned style of preparing the earth for its next arrival.

Then it took Elmer almost six hours to open a grave.

He'd cart up to 26 wheelbarrow loads of dirt out of the ground and put them out of sight. So's the family wouldn't see the big mound that would go back in later and cover over the coffin and vault. Then, after the graveside preachin' and flower tossin', he'd haul the earth back and make things real nice and smooth.

"You get people who go in and slap it out," Elmer said, his voice with a hard edge showing his distaste. "They got no respect for what you do in a cemetery. But I care about those deceased souls. I'm the last one that provides the departed a service. I come in after the undertaker and even after the preacher.

"I like to cut the corners of my graves real sharp. Take pride in my work, I do. 'Cause I like everything to look nice and it makes me feel real good to hear people say: 'That there's a good job by Elmer Tyson.' "

Emma wasn't always working by his side. When they were first married, she used to send him off with his lunch in a bag and hot soup in a Thermos. She'd be home taking care of the kids.

For some reason, though, this one year, she went out to see him. Thought she'd give him a surprise.

He was at an old yard near the shoreline, down on the western water edges of Wicomico County, where the ground was soft and had lots of sand mixed in with the clay.

Elmer, he was working all by his lonesome, and she pulled up their car right next to his truck.

Calling out a few times, she didn't get an answer.

Emma decided to walk around the churchyard, looking in all directions. Then she spotted a mound of earth he had tossed out of the hole and she headed straight for it.

Looking down inside the grave, she let out a short gasp.

Elmer's leg was the first thing she saw. It was sticking out of the dirt. A bit further over was one arm and part of his head, protruding from a pile of loose, dry earth.

The rest of his body was covered with a dusty orange and brown mixture. The side of the freshly dug grave had fallen in. During the struggle to get out, Elmer's body was twisted and, upon losing his balance, his head hit the shovel and he was knocked out.

Emma thanked God for sending her to visit Elmer that day. She knew that had the dirt and sand covered her husband's face, he could have died.

From that day since, Emma went to work with him every day. Wearing a straw gardening hat and loose overalls, she could be found sitting nearby and often looking down, just conversing along as he worked.

She'd work on her sewing or patching, sometimes read a book or just listen to the transistor radio.

Oftentimes, she'd get up and carry a wheelbarrow or two of dirt out of sight, ignoring Elmer when he shouted for her to put it down.

At midday they would share their lunch and talk about what they planned to do when they retired: Take a cruise. Get a place near the beach. Spend money on the grandchildren. Buy a new truck, with a camper on the back, and head out west on a long driving vacation.

Many's the day that Elmer would walk the grounds of the churches and graveyards and pick a clump of wild flowers for Emma. black-eyed Susans were her favorite.

When she wasn't looking, he'd sneak a fresh-picked bouquet onto the passenger's seat of the truck, so she'd be surprised when she opened the door.

At least twice a week Emma would ride home beside Elmer, smiling as she gently held a yellow and black wildflower bouquet in her lap.

Elmer admitted that it took some getting used to, sitting out there alone with the dead.

"Things would come into your mind, all the time at first," he said. "Each little noise you'd hear, you'd stop and look. But it was your imagination making it worse than it was. You could give yourself a heart attack worrying. You're scared and jumpy. It's pitch black. You've got a grave to get open before first light. Morning's on its way, and you're running behind schedule. But the sun, it don't care. It's got to go down and rest. But you, you got to keep digging. And the light from the generator is throwing shadows.

"But you get used to it. It's the living that can hurt you," he'd always say. "The dead, they don't care about you. Only the living can hurt or help you."

One winter, in particular, there was death in the air.

No one was spared—children, grandparents, those in their prime—from the influenza that was makin' the rounds.

Elmer needed to rest but he also had to push himself to keep up with the increase in business.

Unfortunately, it took it's toll on Emma. Caught her real sudden. She picked up a cold at first. Tried to pass it off as nothing.

But it got worse. Came on real quick.

She died, peaceful, in her sleep. At home, near her family like she wanted.

Elmer was right there. Leaned over and gave her a final soft kiss. His best friend was gone.

It was a shock. Real tough on the entire family.

But Elmer had lived with death his whole life. Other than Emma, Death had been his constant companion. It was no stranger.

He let his children take care of the funeral arrangements, but Elmer insisted on digging her grave himself—by hand—the way he was taught when he started so many years ago.

He made it real nice. Took extra care, and knew Emma would approve.

Elmer shed his tears in private. Despite the advice of his children and doctor, he went back to work within days of the funeral.

A full, lonely year went by without Emma, but he spoke to her every day. While he was working he'd talk aloud, about the kids, their grandchildren, the grave digging business and how much he missed her. Elmer asked Emma who she thought would be digging his grave for him, when he was placed beside her in the family plot under the tall shade tree.

It was mid February, the same time of year that Emma died.

Elmer, now nearing 70, was working outside Cambridge, Md.

There was a tall wall all around the church. And the gravesites, well, they was tight together and real old. Entry into the yard was through a tiny iron gate.

Elmer, he knew this one would have to be done by hand.

He was digging a double depth, which means it had to be deeper than the usual, since it would be holdin' a husband and wife who died together in a car wreck. The pair of caskets would be stacked atop each other at burial.

Both Elmer and his grandson, who had just started coming along to help him, were working for several hours when the younger man left to made a quick run to the hardware store, to replace a shovel handle that had just broke.

Elmer was more than 7 feet below the surface when he looked up at the rectangle he had taken out of the Earth, admiring the frame it made beneath the sky. As he focused on the drifting white clouds and blue background, silently, two sides of the grave started to give way.

The dirt was falling, not slowly, but fast, in a rush.

Stunned, his reflexes not what they once were, Elmer started to claw to get out. But, he couldn't match the speed of the silent mound of dirt that was steadily covering his entire body. In less than a minute, Elmer had fallen back and his body and face were covered.

Unable to breath, he stopped fighting the inevitable and let darkness have its way. He was on his way to be with Emma.

He didn't know how long he was unconscious.

Elmer's eyes opened to see his grandson above him, smacking his cheeks, tossing water on his face and rubbing away the dirt.

"Poppop. Poppop! Talk to me!" The boy shouted.

"I'm fine. . . .Okay. . . . " Elmer gasped, spitting the dry dirt from between his lips.

"What happened?" the older man asked. "How long have I been out?"

The boy said he didn't know. He had arrived and discovered the cave-in.

But somehow, the dirt had been pushed away, cleared away

just from Elmer's face, as if someone wanted to make sure he could breath until help came.

There was no one there to take credit, but even Elmer, still laying down, could still see the distinct markings, indicating that a pair of hands had pulled the earth aside and piled it on his chest.

Whoever left the finger marks had saved him from suffocating, had saved Elmer Tyson's life.

As Elmer struggled to climb out of the hole and stand upright, he brushed the dirt from his clothing.

It was then that he and his grandson noticed two, yellow black-eyed Susans fall out onto the ground.

Their bright, sunny color appeared as a dramatic contrast to the cold, damp graveyard dirt.

And that pair of fresh, summer wildflowers stood out, for all to notice, sending a message of undying love through the cold Delmarva winter air to Elmer Tyson—Eastern Shore Gravedigger.

Ed and Kathleen Okonowicz

Ed Okonowicz, a Delaware native, teaches both storytelling and writing classes at area colleges. Kathleen Burgoon Okonowicz, a watercolor artist and illustrator, is originally from Greenbelt, Maryland, and is a signature member of the Baltimore Watercolor Society.

A professional storyteller, Ed presents programs throughout the Mid-Atlantic region. He is a member of the Delaware Humanities Forum Speakers Bureau and Visiting Scholars Program and serves on the Maryland State Arts Council Folk Arts Advisory Panel.

Kathleen enjoys taking things of the past and preserving them in her paintings. Her print, *Special Places*, features the stately stairway in Wilmington, Delaware, that was the "special place" of the characters in Ed's love story, *Stairway over the Brandywine*. In the fall of 1999, she released *Station No. 5*, a print that captures the charm of a 1893 Victorian-style firehouse also in Wilmington, near Trolley Square. In 2002, she released her third print, *The Broom Man*, featuring William Hammond III of Felton, Del., Delmarva's Broom Man, who also is the subject of a chapter in the book *Disappearing Delmarva*.

A graduate of Salisbury State University, Kathleen earned her master's degree in professional writing from Towson State University.

As the owners of Myst and Lace Publishers Inc., Kathleen is responsible for art, photography, layout and design, while Ed conducts the interviews and writes the stories.

For information on storytelling, call Ed. For self-publishing or graphic design assistance, call Kathleen. Telephone: 410 398-5013. Visit their web site: www.mystandlace.com

Myst and Lace Publishers Inc.

Myst and Lace Publishers, Inc. was formed in 1994 during an early evening neighborhood walk. Ed mentioned to Kathleen that he needed to find a "few more" local ghost stories to use during storytelling programs. He had been buying books about ghosts and folklore featuring stories in other states and said, "I bet if we placed a notice that we were seeking ghost stories in the newspaper, we might get two or three responses."

Within a week of the appearance of headlines in several newspapers stating: "Guy Wants Ghosts," they received more than 24 letters and phone calls from people with tales to tell. The result was *Pulling Back the Curtain*, Vol. I of the *Spirits Between the Bays* ghost/folklore series. As the years passed, they kept receiving leads—through the mail, over the phone and at book signings and storytelling events. The series, whose titles led readers through a literary haunted house, continued: through the open Door, into the Vestibule, and Parlor, and Kitchen, up the Back Stairway, into the Hallway and ending in the Bedchamber (with Vol. IX).

Along the way they released two books about the fascinating world of haunted antiques—*Possessed Possessions* and *Possessed Possessions* 2. For obvious reasons you don't usually find these books for sale in antique shops.

The company's proudest achievement came in the summer of 1997, with the release of *Disappearing Delmarva: Portraits of the Peninsula People*. This hardbound, coffeetable-style book with photographs and stories, received two national first-place awards (in both the general book and the photography catagories). During its production, Ed and Kathleen were honored to meet the wonderful people who live on the peninsula and contribute to its regional culture, traditions and folkways.

They've also produced two murder mystery novels—FIRED! and *Halloween House*—set in the fictional state of DelMarVa, featuring "tough on crime" governor Henry McDevitt and police commissioner Michael Pentak. This series and its characters will continue.

Terryfing Tales of the Beaches and Bays and *Terrifying Tales 2*, were popular beach reading volumes in the summers of 2001 and 2002.

A volume of haunted stories, entitled *Ghosts*, which features a photograph of Patty Cannon's skull, was released in the fall of 2001. In the spring of 2002, the company produced a biography of well known Delaware sportswriter Matt Zabitka, entitled *Matt Zabitka SPORTS: 60 Years of Headlines and Deadlines*. This book was written by Ed and his good friend co-author Jerry Rhodes.

Since in 1994, Myst and Lace Publishers has focused on regional topics that both entertain and educate its readers, making them aware of the history, folklore, culture and legends of the region. In each of the books, whether they focus on ghosts, murder or folklore, readers learn interesting facts about Delmarva's fascinating past.

To those of you who have supported them, Ed and Kathleen say, 'Thank you.' If you are a new reader, welcome to their DelMarValous world.

The following pages feature information on our books.
To order, use the form on page 122, go to Amazon.com or
visit the Myst and Lace web site at: www.mystandlace.com

True
Ghost Stories
from Master Storyteller
Ed Okonowicz

*S*pirits
Between the Bays
Series

Volume by volume our haunted house grows.
Enter at your own risk!

Wander through the rooms, hallways and dark corners of this eerie series.

Creep deeper and deeper into terror, and learn about the area's history in our series of ghostly tales and folklore of the Mid-Atlantic region.

"If this collection doesn't give you a chill, check your pulse, you might be dead."

–Leslie R. McNair
The Review, University of Delaware

"This expert storyteller can even make a vanishing hitchhiker story fresh and startling."

–Chris Woodyard
author of *Haunted Ohio* series

POSSESSED OBJECTS PLAGUE THEIR OWNERS

112 pages
5 1/2" x 8 1/2"
softcover
ISBN 0-9643244-5-8

112 pages
5 1/2" x 8 1/2"
softcover
ISBN 0-890690-02-3

$9.95 each

A BUMP. A THUD. MYSTERIOUS MOVEMENT. Unexplained happenings. Caused by What? Venture through this collection of short stories and discover the answer. Experience eerie, true tales about items from across the country that, apparently, have taken on an independent spirit of their own—for they refuse to give up the ghost.

From Maine to Florida, from Pennsylvania to Wisconsin . . haunted heirlooms exist among us . . . everywhere.

Read about them in *Possessed Possessions* and *Possessed Possessions* **2** the books some antique dealers *definitely* do not want you to buy.

"If you're looking for an unusual gift for a collector of antiques, or enjoy haunting tales, this one's for you."
—Collector Editions

"This book is certainly entertaining, and it's even a bit disturbing."
—Antique Week

". . . an intriguing read."
—Maine Antique Digest

WARNING
There could be more than just dust hovering around some of the items in your home.

www.mystandlace.com

... *and you thought sharks were the only danger at the beach!*

In *Terrifying Tales of the Beaches and Bays* and the sequel, *Terrifying Tales 2 of the Beaches and Bays*, award-winning author and storyteller Ed Okonowicz shares eerie accounts of spirits roaming the shore.

Read about:

- A river pilot's memorable New Year's Eve cruise

- Desperate Confederates escaping from an island prison

- Serious seekers of pirate gold

- Fishermen stranded in the icy Chesapeake Bay

- Lighthouse keepers still tending long-gone beacon

- Hauntings near the Indian River Life Saving Station

- A most unusual "catch of the day"

- Ocean City's "Trash Rat"

- The legend of Bigg Lizz . . . . and more . . . .

128 pages
5 1/2" x 8 1/2"
softcover
ISBN 1-890690-06-6
$9.95

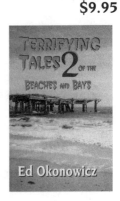

128 pages
5 1/2" x 8 1/2"
softcover
ISBN 1-890690-10-4
$9.95

**Popular Delmarva
summer beach reading
in 2001 and 2002**

Ghosts

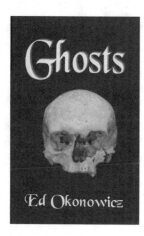

112 pages
5 1/2" x 8 1/2"
softcover
ISBN 0-890690-08-2

$9.95

Ghosts

Nearly 40% of Americans believe in ghosts.

Find out why, in this collection of true tales and eerie fiction, featuring

• Five college football players who flee their ghost infested apartment,
• Troubled homes in Lewes, Del., and near the site of a New Jersey Revolutionary War massacre,
• A haunted supermarket, ghost dog, phantom military car, haunted barn and the Pig Woman legend,

. . . and more.

Treasure Hunting
Seek and You Shall Find

by
Eddie Okonowicz

(son of author Ed Okonowicz)

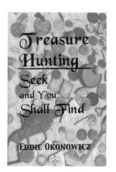

48 pages
5 1/2" x 8 1/2"
softcover
ISBN 1-890690-07-4

$6.95

Loaded with:

Tips on using a metal detector to hunt for relics and treasure, plus
Photos of numerous historical finds.

www.mystandlace.com

The DelMarVa Murder Mystery series

FIRED!

Early in the 21st century, DelMarVa, the newest state in the union, which includes Delaware and the Eastern Shore of Maryland and Virginia, is plagued by a ruthless serial killer. In FIRED! meet Gov. Henry McDevitt, Police Commissioner Michael Pentak and State Psychologist Stephanie Litera as they track down the peninsula's worst killer since 19th century murderess Patty Cannon.

Ed Okonowicz

320 pages
4 1/4" x 6 3/4"
softcover
ISBN 1-890690-01-5
$9.95

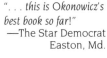

WELCOME to the State of DelMarVa

"Politics and romance make fairly strange bedfellows, but add a dash of mystery and mahem and the result can be spectacular, as evidenced in FIRED!"
—Sharon Galligar Chance
BookBrowser Review

"Lots of familiar places in this imaginative suspense novel."
—Jeannine Lahey
About.com
Wilmington, Del.

". . . this is Okonowicz's best book so far!"
—The Star Democrat
Easton, Md.

Halloween House

In Halloween House, the series continues as Gov. McDevitt, Commissioner Pentak and other DelMarVa crime fighters go up against Craig Dire, a demented businessman who turns his annual Halloween show into a real-life chamber of horrors.

Ed Okonowicz

320 pages
4 1/4" x 6 3/4"
softcover
ISBN 1-890690-03-1
$9.95

Delaware Press Association
First Place Award
2000

"Halloween House mystery chills summer heat."
—Rosanne Pack
Cape Gazette

"Looking at the front cover, the reader knows it's going to be a bumpy night."
—Erika Quesenbery
The Herald

Disappearing Delmarva
Portraits of the Peninsula People

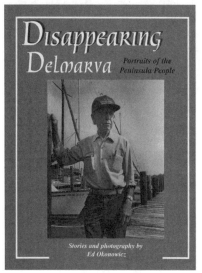

Photography and stories
by Ed Okonowicz

Disappearing Delmarva introduces
you to more than 70 people on the
peninsula whose professions are
endangered. Their work, words
and wisdom are captured in the
208 pages of this hardbound volume, which features more than 60
photographs.

Along the back roads and back
creeks of Delaware, Maryland, and
Virginia—in such hamlets as
Felton and Blackbird in Delaware, Taylors
Island and North East in Maryland, and
Chincoteague and Sanford in Virginia—these colorful residents still work at the trades that have
been passed down to them by grandparents and
elders.

208 pages
8 1/2" x 11"
Hardcover
ISBN 1-890690-00-7

$38.00

Winner of 2 First-Place Awards:

Best general book
Best Photojournalism entry

National Federation of Press Women Inc.
1998 Communication Contest

Ed presents a program based on this award-winning book at local
historical societies and libraries. Contact him at 410 398-5013 to arrange
a program in your area.

Matt Zabitka: Sports
60 Years of Headlines and Deadlines

by Ed Okonowicz and Jerry Rhodes

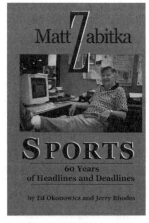

Since his first hand-written column for
ester's *Progressive Weekly* at age 13, Matt
:e" Zabitka has been associated with profes-
nal, scholastic and amateur sports. In more
n 10,000 columns, Zee has shared his con-
rsations with sports' greatest legends and he
s recorded the achievements of local heroes.

This book features scores of Matt's favorite
periences and more than 35 columns, which
has selected—including interviews with Joe
Maggio, Stan Musial, "Boom Boom" Mancini,
d Williams, Goose Goslin and Ralph Kiner.

There also are columns about local athletes
s a section spotlighting Delawareans who
yed in the Negro National Baseball League.

Read about Matt's personal correspondence
h Ty Cobb, his stint as a radio show host and
experiences as a sought after toastmaster.

224 pages	over 30 photographs
6" x 9"	ISBN 1-890690-09-0
hardbound	**$24.95**

Following 10 years at the *Chester Times*, the "classic" sportswriter joined
e *News Journal* in 1962 and has never stopped writing.

This hardbound book will be a collector's item.

Iatt, as described by others in the field of sports

*"When I first met him, he immediately struck me as the classic sportswriter. If
ey were going to do a movie about Matt's life, it's a shame that Walter Matthau
ied, because he could play Matt—with a cigar hanging halfway out of his
outh, banging on a typewriter, talking on the phone and working late into the
ight."* **—Kevin Tresolini,** sportswriter, *The News Journal*

*"Every city of any size needs a Matt Zabitka, who I respectfully call a chroni-
er, someone who has a history and   picture of the past. You need someone with
ep roots in the community. Wilmington is fortunate to have that in Matt."*
—Pat Williams, senior vice president, Orlando Magic

*"He made you feel comfortable, and he made me feel important. He's been
ind to me and he's always covered my career in a positive way. That means a lot
me. He's a really good guy."*
—Randy White, former defensive tackle for the Dallas Cowboys

To complete your collection. . .
or to tell us about *your* ghostly experience, use the form below:

Name _____

Address_____

City_____State_____Zip Code_____

Phone Numbers _(_____)_____(_____)_____
                        Day   Evening

To receive the free *Spirits Speaks* newsletter and information on future volumes, visit our web site [www.mystandlace.com] or fill out the above form and mail it to us.

I would like to order the following books:

Quantity	Title	Price	Total
_____	Matt Zabitka: Sports	$24.95	_____
_____	Ghosts	$ 9.95	_____
_____	Pulling Back the Curtain, Vol I	$ 8.95	_____
_____	**Opening the Door, Vol II (second edition)**	**$ 9.95**	_____
_____	Welcome Inn, Vol III	$ 8.95	_____
_____	In the Vestibule, Vol IV	$ 9.95	_____
_____	Presence in the Parlor, Vol V	$ 9.95	_____
_____	Crying in the Kitchen, Vol VI	$ 9.95	_____
_____	Up the Back Stairway, Vol VII	$ 9.95	_____
_____	Horror in the Hallway, Vol VIII	$ 9.95	_____
_____	Phantom in the Bedchamber, Vol IX	$ 9.95	_____
_____	Terrifying Tales of the Beaches and Bays	$ 9.95	_____
_____	Terrifying Tales 2 of the Beaches and Bays	$ 9.95	_____
_____	Possessed Possessions	$ 9.95	_____
_____	Possessed Possessions 2	$ 9.95	_____
_____	Fired! A DelMarVa Murder Mystery(DMM)	$ 9.95	_____
_____	Halloween House DMM#2	$ 9.95	_____
_____	Disappearing Delmarva	$38.00	_____
_____	Stairway over the Brandywine, A Love Story	$ 5.00	_____
_____	Treasure Hunting	$ 6.95	_____

*Md residents add 5% sales tax.
Please include $2.00 postage for the first book, and 50 cents for each additional book.
Make checks payable to:
Myst and Lace Publishers

Subtotal_____
Tax*_____
Shipping_____
Total_____

All books are signed by the author. If you would like the book(s) personalized, please specify to whom.

Mail to: Ed Okonowicz
1386 Fair Hill Lane
Elkton, Maryland 21921
www.mystandlace.com